REDEMPTION

ALY SEBASTIAN

FOR JAMES

I love you.

-To Rowan, Persephone and Karick for whom this book is inappropriate for at this time: Dysgraphia hasn't stopped me from loving or writing books. Don't let anyone make you think you are less or can do less. You are so much more.   Even when the world is unfair or breaks you to pieces, you can look within and create a new one from the shards.

ACKNOWLEDGMENTS

A big thanks to my husband Jay. Thanks to my children Persephone, Rowan and Karick who pushed me to do better and be better and who told me I should be a writer. Thanks to my mom whose nose was in a book so much that I had to find out what the fuss was about. Thanks to my dad who told me stories every night and who had me type out his own book. Thanks to my Grampy who loved books and said that someone in the family better be a writer. Thanks to my aunt who had a huge stash of romance novels at her house. Thanks to V.L. for listening to me talk about writing incessantly. Thanks to Chanda Tan who told me I better fucking publish this thing. Thanks to Richie Bettencourt for being so supportive and willing to help especially with all the tech stuff.

Thanks to all the other writers I know that aren't actually writing. I didn't want to be one of you anymore. Thanks to Brenna Lyons for coming into my life at the right time to show me what I wasn't doing. Thanks to my thirties that kick started me into a panic mode over what I was contributing to the world and the need to immortalize myself. Thanks to all those who didn't help with this book when they said they would and to those who refused when asked. I didn't need your support anyway.

ALY SEBASTIAN

PROLOGUE

He watched her swat the lock of hair from the delicate curve of her gamine face. She was so deep in concentration that she didn't realize she had smeared red across her temple that appeared as if a bloody gash. His fingers ached to wipe it away for her. He knew from the frenzy in which her hands worked that she had no thought whatsoever to appearance or her surroundings. The world had fallen away and the only thing that existed was her, the paint and the large canvas in front of her. She looked as if she stood in the eye of some storm that she herself was raising like some wild and fey creature from a place outside of space and time. Her only acknowledgement that she did, in fact, exist on this plane was to flick on a large light when the sun faded.

It was almost dawn. She had been at it for hours without a break. She seemed to be fueled by the need to create, gaining momentum with each brush stroke and that need overrode all required functions of the body save breathing. That breath was coming out almost like that of sleep, slow and deep from parted lips although her hands and arms worked furiously. He didn't stay long enough to see what happened when that energy was all used up. Didn't want to see her vulnerable. Didn't want to think of what may happen when all her guards were down due to sheer exhaustion. He shook his head at the thought. *No.* He said to himself silently. He got up from his perch on her windowsill and soundlessly disappeared into the last dregs of night.

"...Love has within it a redemptive power. And there is a power there that eventually transforms individuals." –Dr. Martin Luther King Jr.

CHAPTER 1

Megan woke up sprawled in her bed. She was lying on her stomach with her pale legs spread out in a V and her arms were crammed beneath her down-filled pillow as though to squeeze it into submission. The sheet was in a tangle around her and her normally smooth skin was covered in gooseflesh. *Why was she cold?* Her tired brain was trying to make sense of her surroundings. *Oh.* She must have left the window open the night before. Must have thrown it wide to let in the September air although she couldn't remember doing so. Memory lapses while working were normal for her so she paid it no heed other than to make a mental note to check the windows each night as it would only be getting cooler and wouldn't want to suffer hypothermia as she slept.

She pushed her messy hair out of her face and glared at the alarm clock as if it meant to spite her. The red numbers on the screen warned that it was past noon. She groaned and rolled into a sitting position in one graceful movement and contemplated going back to sleep but decide that was impossible. She had to get up.

She rose letting the sheet drop, giving no thought to her nudity as she walked to the open window. A breeze puckered her nipples and she reached up and yanked down the heavy sash until it thunked against the sill.

She picked her way over to the big Queen Anne chair in the corner of the bedroom next to her closet. It was heaped with the clean laundry that never quite made it to her overstuffed dresser. She dug out a pair of faded jeans and a t-shirt and threw them on without actually looking at them.

Occasionally, when doing this she'd put pants over her head and spent a good ten minutes trying to find the hole for her head. She would've laughed but was too tired. As long as she had on a top and bottom that covered her top and bottom it didn't matter if they matched. Almost all of her clothes were black which made it easy for her on days like this when she was a total zombie. She didn't bother with a bra or underwear unless absolutely necessary and this day was no exception although she grabbed a flannel shirt to at least cover the hard tips of her breasts that pushed against the thin cotton of her tee.

Once dressed, she padded over to the bathroom to brush her teeth and to roll up her mass of wily black hair into a big messy bun before dabbing on some burgundy lipstick. She darted her eyes at the mirror just in case. Satisfied she was at least presentable, meaning she didn't have a clown face or lipstick in her teeth or a sock or pair of panties stuck in her hair, which had happened once, she grabbed her boots from beneath the bed and headed to the door.

She was careful not to look at the big canvas in the middle of the room. It wasn't yet draped with a cloth and the spotlight shone down on it to help it dry. Luckily it faced east so that she'd have to be on the other side of the room to catch a glimpse. That was *not* what she wanted.

The painting definitively was her pink elephant in the room and she had no desire to face it at that moment. She tried to keep her eyes focused on a large pottery vase in the corner to keep herself from peeking. She counted the petals on the hand-painted red flowers that snaked up its glossy blue sides all the way to the rim as she maneuvered her way around the furniture by memory.

Once she had made her way over to what she thought of as enemy territory, the west side of the room, she sighed and closed her eyes. She would not look, she told herself. She stubbed her toe on the way to the closet that held her coat and bag, swearing a streak of almost unintelligible obscenities mixed with random everyday words that she hadn't already put her boots on and instead had carried them from her bedroom. She needed coffee. Bad.

She grabbed the buttery leather coat and the matching saddle bag if that's what you would call it. The purse was actually more fabric with leather trim and of a larger scale than the chic little motorcycle jacket and was large enough to carry just about anything Megan needed throughout her day. Her friends called it her Mary Poppin's bag due to the things she pulled from its depths ranging from the strange, the practical, to the completely ridiculous. Finding necessities in its chaos was another thing altogether. She locked up and threw her keys into the abyss.

The two blocks to the little coffee house were effortless. Megan could walk it in her sleep and was sure she had a few times. She could smell the coffee and pastries from the moment she stepped out of her door and the sweet aroma pulled her along to its source like in one of those old cartoons with the trail of scent you could see on the air that lifted and carried the character along with it. She pulled her sunglasses from her coat pocket, crammed them on her face and began walking briskly. She took a deep breath and imagined herself in Paris although she'd never been.

The air was cool and underneath the bakery scents, she could smell the leaves turning. It was hard to describe the earthy, crisp decaying smell that spoke to her soul. She always loved autumn in Massachusetts. Soon the streets would be lined in crimson and pumpkin and gold and that magical scent would be released with each crunching step she took. It was heaven on earth.

With a large coffee in one hand and a huge blueberry muffin stuffed in her bag, she set off on the walk back to her Cambridge apartment. She was going to take the long way; past the train station and through the park. She wanted some time to wake up before she went home to face the canvas in her studio.

That to her was the hardest part of being an artist. Judging her own work was an agonizing task. She always thought it wasn't good enough and sometimes it really wasn't. Not for her at least. She had trained at the prestigious Museum of Fine Arts College and should know quality art. If it was good it would go to the posh little gallery that sold her work for her and she could make rent this month. If it wasn't, well, she'd have to whitewash the canvas and try not to think of the astronomical cost of the paint she wasted and do something a little more saleable. Her problem was that because of her classical training she compared hers to the work of masters and of course, she was no Michelangelo.

She wound her way through the park and sat on her favorite bench and took a few swigs of creamy French Vanilla coffee from her giant Styrofoam cup. It burned her tongue a little as it slid down but the jolt of caffeine coursing through her made her sigh with relief.

Paper ruffled in the breeze as she grabbed her sketchbook and a charcoal pencil from her bag and began to draw, letting the peace of the day settle on her shoulders and flow through her hands.

She sketched the ducks in the pond as they dunked their feathery heads beneath the grimy surface over and over in an ungraceful search for lunch. Soon they'd be gone, headed to somewhere warmer until spring. She would miss them.

With careful strokes, she drew the arch of the small footbridge that was at least one hundred years old, its underside completely covered in graffiti that made a sharp, modern statement on the historic cobbles.

Finally, Megan turned her attention to a homeless man asleep on a bench across from where she sat and began to bring him to life on the paper in front of her. She lovingly drew the deep creases on his face that made him seem ageless. Felt the cold with him as she drew the contours of layers of grimy clothes that covered his thin frame, his only defense against the cruel and fickle New England weather. She captured the desolation of the moment. The sadness of the situation, a man alone with nothing and no one aside from the ducks, ignorant of all except their own search for food. It was hard to impart a feeling into a sketch but in that was where her talent way. She had the uncanny ability to convey emotion in two dimension while using very realistic detail. It was type of

Impressionism mixed with Realism that was rarely seen any more if ever.

She decided to do a full landscape and add in the slumbering man. She'd just leave him on the bench amidst the beautiful yet subtly corrupt scenery. She'd call him the invisible man since so many people consider these lost souls just part of the scenery. No one really saw them as people. More like an obstacle to be avoided and not like the suffering humans they were. It was unfair but part of life in the city. Her fellow Bostonians rarely dipped they're hands into the pockets of their expensive suits and handbags to produce the change that was begged for on almost every corner. She did what she could and this tribute would send a subtle message to its viewers. No one liked their callousness thrown in their faces.

When she roughly finished the outline sketch of her little cityscape, Megan got up and stretched before she walked over to the other bench. Her unwitting subject curled up in the haven of sleep though he looked as though he did not find peace even there. She reached into her huge purse and took out the paper bag with the muffin in it and placed it beside him with the remains of the still warm coffee and turned to walk home.

She found her courage that she had been missing all morning somewhere along the way, possibly from the reality that her problems at the moment were insignificant in the larger scheme of things. Embracing this momentary new perspective, Megan deliberately adjusted her stride from the leisurely stroll of the last block to long confident strides.

She was ready to face her work.

It seemed that every step back toward her apartment led her back down the road of apprehension. She was just wondering how she'd muster up the courage once more when Megan was saved by the bell. The phone in her purse was ringing. It was the sound of an old telephone that you might find in an English phone booth, not in someone's bag. After stopping to dig for a few minutes she found it and managed to answer before the tone stopped and it went to voicemail. "Hi Mom", she said breathlessly.

The woman on the other end seemed surprised she answered. It took her a minute to adjust from what she had planned to say to a machine to how to actually greet her daughter. Almost always the phone went straight to the messaging service.

"Hi, Love," the breathy voice finally spoke. Josephine Black had a voice like blue velvet.

"What's up?" Megan asked warily, not sure if she actually wanted an answer.

She wondered, as she usually did if her mom was drunk and thus the reason for the call. It was the woman's usual state and she liked to call out of nowhere when she was hitting the bottle and leave a dozen or so messages. These ranged from highly emotional guilty apologies to screaming that Megan was a terrible daughter who ruined her life. Nothing different with her mother. She heard the same things over and over from her as a child.

Megan looked at the time on the phone. It was two in the afternoon so it was definitely a possibility that Josephine was in a black, whiskey inspired mood. She was brought out of her wayward thoughts by her mother's silky voice sounding completely sober if not a bit agitated.

"Can ya come down ta the pub tonight? I've been needin' ta talk ta ya," she asked.

Shit! This was not good. Megan could feel herself scowling. The only time Megan's mom asked to talk to her it was to ask for something. Money, a ride to some random place for god knows what reason. Bail.

She loved her Ma but she was just so draining. She did not have the energy for this today. Her nerves were already stretched tight. She thought quickly trying to figure out a way to end this phone call as quickly and painlessly as possible with no chance for her mother to have a reason to hound her. Her chances didn't look good but she decided to cross her fingers and wing it.

"How about tomorrow?" it wasn't a question, "Say two o'clock?" she would be locked in if her mother agreed but there was no getting around it.

She knew she had time the next day but hoped this was just a check-in. Her mother often checked in with her after a long bender of drunkenness to assuage her guilt and assure herself nothing happened in the world while she was out of it. That the show went on without her but that she was sorely missed.

Josephine seemed a little taken aback by her daughter's abruptly cold tone and cleared her throat so her nerves wouldn't be heard in her voice.

She took the offensive, "Weel, I was hoping t'would be today but I guess I'm lucky ya even bothered ta answer yer phone ta talk ta yer *Mother*," this last was said with a thick accent so it sounded like *Mudder*.

Josephine's Irish was up. It only took five seconds. Megan had counted. Not that it took too much to make the older woman angry. She was used to getting her way and wouldn't stop at being petty to get it but at the moment Megan had bigger fish to fry.

"Listen, Ma," she sounded apologetic as she could. In truth, Megan was exasperated at having to skirt a confrontation before she even had a full cup of coffee but she refused to let her mother goad her into another argument which would ultimately leave her feeling guilty, frustrated, and like a terrible person. Then she'd have to go down and apologize to ease her conscience for losing her temper and that would give the older woman exactly what she wanted. Instant gratification. She hated the way the older woman could manipulate her so easily. *Well, not today!* Megan thought.

She made her voice sweet though she spoke quickly, "I'm working today, I have a few things to take care of over here. I'll be there tomorrow at two," if she didn't put any air in the conversation she might get out of this, "I love you. I'll see you tomorrow. I gotta run Ma. Bye."

Megan slid her finger across the screen to end the call and shut the ringer off. She threw it back in her purse like it might bite her hand. *Great,* she thought. She would have rather made an appointment to get hit with a bus at two and seriously contemplated making it happen for a moment. She was so shocked by her own thoughts that she laughed as an MBTA bus whooshed by her as if she had wished it into existence.

Megan undid the series of locks on the scarred front door. After refastening them all behind her she ran up the stairs, flung her keys on the little side table and threw her jacket and bag in the general direction of the closet. She didn't bother to take off her boots, thinking of her big toe that still smarted from that morning. In her present mood, she may have kicked something so it was safer with them on.

Megan averted her gaze from the large rectangle taking up most of her studio and went to the tiny kitchenette. Her courage and determination from earlier were spent after her short conversation with Josephine. She'd need to gain back some perspective.

She picked up the cold coffeepot containing yesterday's coffee and poured a cup. She wrinkled her nose at the bitter taste, almost regretting leaving her cup of French vanilla with the man on the bench.

Unconsciously, she shrugged to herself, "So much

for breakfast," she said into the cup.

It was two thirty and she was starving. She gulped down as much of the disgusting swill as she could without it coming back up, and put the cup in the already full sink.

She stood looking out the window at the people bustling by a few streets over. Then over to the small cathedral close to the park. It was the only building in Boston like it. The architecture was to die for. French Gothic in an homage to Notre Dame. It always seemed like a shame to her that it was forced to close its doors like so many others that had to in recent years due to law suits, budgets, and poor attendance. Megan imagined the building as being a silent observer much like the gargoyles that flanked its portico that she thought of as neighbors. She named them Mike and Ike. The thought of the statues as old friends was heartening and studying their regal serenity finally brought her back to feeling somewhat calmer and more centered.

With a look of longing, she stared at the fridge hoping something delicious like a four course meal had appeared in its depths while she was out.

"Yeah right," she muttered aloud and opened the door. Not surprisingly, as the little lightbulb lit up the inside she could see that it was almost completely empty inside.

Megan sighed wistfully and grabbed a coke and a box of leftover Chinese. She straightened her spine and slowly walked back to the main room.

She was digging into the white cardboard container viciously with her fork like a starved lunatic, hoping to push down the butterflies rising up in her stomach with the noodles she was shoving in her mouth. After choking down nearly half of the cold Lo Mein, she washed it down with the soda and plopped ungracefully on the little couch directly in front of the canvas.

Swallowing the last of the greasy leftovers along with the lump in her throat, she took a deep breath and looked up. The scene in front of her was of the city beyond her windows. A dark study of tall glassy buildings interspersed with shorter, older, more ornate ones. Asphalt sidewalks and cobbled parks. She chewed slowly as she got up to take a closer look. It was all shaded with the tones of nightfall with the subtle warm glow from lamp posts, doorways, and the occasional window. The scene swept from street to structure encompassing all with an air of mystery. Of secrets behind windows and doors, shadows lurking behind and inside buildings, battling with the small glowing lights of those still awake, wary of what was happening.

That's funny, she thought as she leaned in closer. She noticed something on the corner of one of the old buildings, it looked like the abandoned church she was just gazing at moments before. There, perched on top of the entryway looking up directly to her, was a man. She couldn't remember painting him there. This was supposed to be a cityscape and though she liked to add people in an almost Where's Waldo type way, she didn't paint this man deliberately and setting him practically on a church roof was pretty weird even for her. There simply wasn't much fantasy in her art. She squinted closer to see if it was just a mistake or a gargoyle or trick of the light. It wasn't. She really couldn't even remember sketching him before and she pretty much remembered everything she saw. She had an eidetic memory.

Megan rose all the way off the faded green velveteen sofa and bent her head so that her nose was almost touching the canvas. She couldn't quite make out his face. The figure was only about an inch tall at most, being scaled with the buildings. He appeared to have longish, dark hair and was perched against a balustrade on the flying buttress of the old structure. He peered up like he was watching her. A chill ran down her spine but she shrugged it off. It would work. Just another hidden picture within a picture.

Satisfied and relieved that the painting was viable for sale, Megan picked up the small brush from the jar of black paint on the messy little table and deftly added her name to the corner. Megan Black in arcs and scrolls so that you could only make out the M and B in the corner. She grabbed the drop cloth from the floor and shook it out before flinging it over the top of the frame, shutting out the darkened city and the watcher from her mind. She'd call the gallery in the morning to send someone to pick it up. Megan felt like celebrating.

After throwing away the rest of her make-do lunch and reminding herself she needed to hit up the market at some point, she gave a call to her best friend Gayle and left a message that she was in the mood to party and asked if she could tag along with her and Diane. She was sure the couple would have plans already and they were *always* together but what was one more really. She'd take a chance. There was nothing worse than celebrating alone on a Friday night. It made her think of lonely old ladies with dozens of cats and pink chintz furniture and thought about how many times she considered getting a kitten from a shelter and shuddered.

Megan spent the next hour cleaning up her apartment which meant picking up stuff off the floor and chairs and shoving it into closets and throwing stuff onto the end of her bed. Gale hadn't taken too long to get back to her saying, of course, she could play the third wheel and that they were going to the Stingray club and that they'd stop at her place first so they could walk up.

"Yay! I can't wait!" she'd said into the receiver and hung up.

She was so elated to be going out with her dearest friends, Megan practically skipped to her room overcome with a mix of excitement at the thought of girl-time and dancing and the joy of selling her painting. Or at least having one to sell.

With a rush of caffeine and giddiness, she dug through the mess of clothes she had just finished stuffing in her closet trying to find something fitting to wear. She flung a few selections on the bedspread, creating a mound of black silks and laces and whatnot until she struck gold toward the back. What she found was a tiny leather dress, black of course, with a square neck and plunging back, a remnant of the 80's. She threw it on the top of the pile she had made on the foot of the bed. Satisfied that would do the best, she grabbed a couple of clean towels and went into the bathroom.

She set the water to as hot as it would go without burning her fair skin and stepped into the old claw-foot tub and shut the curtain. She loved that tub. The enamel was worn and the brass was in serious need of polishing but there was beauty in the antiquity of it. She had painted the outside of it with trailing vines of roses to cover up where it had peeled. Megan would've loved to live in a time when everything was crafted in such ornate detail. She wasn't one for modern lines and sleek utilitarian simplicity. She loved antiques and vintage clothes. Everything was so artfully made in Victorian times and the eras before, unlike the stuff she found in stores recently. It all was so angular and ergonomic and cold, not to mention cheaply made. She needed carved wood, hand painted silk, tapestry, scrolling, and gilt.

Megan hummed an old Gaelic lullaby while she washed her hair and shaved her legs. She stood for a long time letting the hot water run down her hair and face and body, basking the feeling of liquid warmth. She was content and calm. Today was definitely not as bad as she'd thought it would end up, all things considered.

Megan stood naked on a towel in front of the medicine cabinet mirror as she brushed and blew dry her long shiny hair. After trying to put it up a few times and cursing the fact that bobby pins couldn't hold the heavy tresses up without them trying to escape, she settled for wearing it down in thick waves like a cape across her shoulders and back. She applied some smoky black liner around her eyes, making her green irises seem even greener, and added some of her signature burgundy lipstick. It was called Brocade. She didn't need any foundation or powder since her skin was clear and milky white but she did sweep some pink blush over her cheeks. The touch of color helped give her a healthy glow. She did not have a complexion that could tolerate too much sun and sometimes she just looked washed out. She was definitely a winter. Satisfied with the effect she padded silently over the glossy walnut floor into her bedroom.

She liked living in her old building with its historic touches and big windows that let in both the sunlight and the moonlight. It was three floors up with an empty storefront beneath her and nothing but some smaller businesses that didn't obstruct her view of the park and St. Augustine's and the city beyond. Megan felt like she had the entire block all to herself. She could prowl the apartment nude with no fear of some pervert watching her from below or from some other building since they all closed at five o'clock thanks to the Blue Laws. She could also work whatever hours she pleased without much interruption, just the sound of the normal cadence of the city or blare her music at all hours without fear of some irate neighbor calling the cops. It was perfect for her. It was home.

Megan donned the supple little leather dress and slathered some lotion on her pale legs before stepping into the ultra-sexy studded black stilettos and buckled the wide leather cuffs that went around her ankles.

She clip-clopped into her studio to get a look in the large mirror that leaned against the far wall. If she was objective she would say she looked sexy, beautiful even. Her raven hair fell in silky undulations down her exposed back and the form fitting dress looked like a second skin. It melded to her firm breasts and small waist and ended slightly above mid-thigh. Her white legs looked longer with the short length of the skirt and tapered down gracefully to the shoes which could not be described as anything but "fuck me pumps". She'd fit in just fine at the club tonight, unlike when she went to some of the other clubs and bars on the ultra-trendy Lansdowne Street. There the girls were tanned and blonde and clad in shimmery little stretchy dresses that made it hard to imagine how they stayed inside of them. Their shoes would mostly be metallic platform spiky things that looked painful to wear. They all looked like super tanned six foot tall Barbie dolls and most of them were on the prowl for rich men. The music there would be techno/hip-hop and butts would be shaking to the beat and drunk girls would be slung over super muscular guys in tight t-shirts and black slacks wearing too much cologne. *Yuck.*

If she was going to go dancing she so preferred the underground Stingray. They hosted a series of themed nights geared toward the subculture of Boston that just didn't want to spend their nights in the uncomfortable "mainstream". There was 80's Night and Fetish Night, Drag Night and Goth Night. Tonight was Friday night. Megan's favorite; Hell Night.

CHAPTER 2

Gayle gave a little honk of the horn before parking in the ever vacant spot reserved for Megan, even though she didn't have a car, and the two women opened the doors and got out. Megan waved at them through the glass and quirked a smile at the pair. Gayle as always looked beautiful. She was supermodel tall and built like it. She had a classically beautiful face and short spiky platinum hair. This week the tips of it were pink. She was wearing skintight shiny pants that looked like they were painted on and a fishnet shirt over a lime green bra. *That girl can pull off anything!* Megan thought with no bitterness but simple wonder.

Gayle's partner was also dressed for clubbing in an outfit that screamed that she was forced, probably literally, into it. The shorter woman's full figure was squeezed into a red satin corset with black lace that gave her a huge mass of squished cleavage. She was also wearing a tiny black lace petticoat thing over leggings. Her hair was down and she had severe bangs that made her look like a 50's pinup. Her boots were tall patent leather with buckles all the way up to her thick calves. The entire look was funny on her simply because it was so out of character. She normally wore severe suits in every shade of brown there was. This was a complete 180. She was kind of Mae West meets Lady Gaga. Megan couldn't help but giggle as she watched the squat lawyer make her way up the walk looking like an angry prostitute.

Megan had roomed with Gayle freshman and sophomore year of college in the dorms and senior year in an apartment, the apartment where Megan still lived although she never bothered to get another roommate. They had been best friends since the first day they arrived at orientation, both terrified but refusing to let it show. Both were wearing mall-bought gothic dresses and combat boots. Kindred spirits. When they found out they were sharing a dorm room it couldn't have been more perfect. Gayle's exuberance and flair balanced out Megan's quiet seriousness they each brought out those qualities in each other.

Another thing that Megan loved about her friend was

that in all the year since they'd know each other, Gayle never let it be known if she had noticed that they came from entirely different worlds. The two were both Bostonians, but Gayle's parents were the type who had a vacation home on the cape, although Megan was always welcome there, and Megan's background didn't allow for vacations at all. Gayle's mother was the attorney general for the state and Megan's was a barmaid. Gayle's father was a high powered CEO and Megan's father…well, she'd never met him. He died before she was born. She was comfortable for the first time in her life letting someone see what her home life really was and Gayle had helped her find the humor in it all. Despite their dissimilarities, or maybe because of them, the two women had formed a friendship that both proclaimed on graduation day would last forever.

Since then, Gayle had worked hard to make her own way in the world on her own terms. Both of her parents pushed their only child to become an attorney but Gayle had chosen art school and after discovering four years later that she lacked the talent, went on to Harvard's School of Business post grad.

It was there that she met Diane. It was instant dislike at first sight. The two could not have been more different. Diane was very straight-laced and driven and Gayle was, well, Gayle. They made a cute couple. Diane was a lawyer who worked in big business contracts. Her usual uniform was a brown wool suit that made her look like a potato. It went well with her brown bob haircut. All business and Gayle ran the gallery that sold Megan's work which made her Megan's sometimes boss, sometimes agent. It was a definite perk since it was so hard to be in the business of being a professional artist and Megan was extremely proud of her friend for following her passions so bravely.

Gayle burst through the door as if she still lived there and gave her bestie a big hug. Diane came in behind her on the stairs looking like she was having a hard time in the tall boots. She pushed past Gayle made her way inside and plopped down heavily on the sofa.

"As you can see this is your friend's work," she heaved breathlessly, sweeping a hand in the air from head to toe. She tried to appear put out but the look of love that shone on her face as she gazed at the offender belied her secret pleasure.

"You look gorgeous hon," Gayle whipped her head around and flashed a dazzling smile.

She still had Megan's shoulders and whispered down to her,"You better not say a word and stop looking at me like that. If you make that face I'm going to laugh and then you're going to laugh and Diane is going to cry, so cut it out!"

Megan pretended to look offended but could barely hide her smirk. Megan was careful not to look her best friend in the eye or she would have burst out in giggles right there on the spot. Megan sucked the humor back down and screwed on a straight face. They let go of each other after a minute. That's when Gayle saw it. She strode to the center of the room and put her hands on her hips. She looked like a pissed off Amazon queen.

"And what do we have here?" she quirked a thick brow at Megan, her hand thrust out to the covered canvas, "Is this why you decided to call your dearest friend after two weeks of being incommunicado to celebrate with you?" she sounded angry and amused.

She knew a new painting was *exactly* why her friend had called her. Megan did not believe in play while she was working. She tapped her foot on the floor impatiently. Megan knew her cue. Everything was a drama with Gayle and the blonde relished being the director.

Megan walked over to the canvas and pulled the cloth down like a magician performing a trick, "Da-da-da-da!" she sang.

She heard a gasp from Diane. She couldn't tell if it was with pleasure or if the poor girl's corset was laced too tight. Megan braced herself and watched as her friend studied the piece. She could feel the sweat forming under her arms as she watched Gayle's shrewd blue eyes scanning the picture, assessing and calculating.

"Are you sending this to the gallery?" she asked suddenly.

"You tell me," it wasn't really a question, Megan was waiting for an approval.

Gayle was silent leaving Megan to answer the question. She was always pushing her to be more assertive.

Megan sighed and said, "I was planning on calling and having Billy pick it up tomorrow."

Gayle didn't let the implacable boss-lady face slide for even a split second, "Good. I can probably get you twenty thousand for this one."

Megan didn't realize she was holding her breath until it all came out of her in a whoosh. She shot her friend a hard look to see if she was kidding. Gayle usually never joked about art or business, unless you counted the odd trendy art show where people came and bought things like a dirty sneaker nailed to a board and called something like "Mother". That kind of art they made fun of with evil relish.

Megan stole a glance at Diane who was leaning back on the sofa with her hand over her generous expanse of exposed chest, looking awestruck. At *her* artwork.

Doubtfully, Megan turned to look again at the painting. She had only given it a cursory once over earlier and then only gave real focus to a small corner where the figure of the man was. She hadn't actually *looked* at it. Not as a whole. Not objectively.

In the night it did look better. Almost like the city was alive. As if you could feel the people asleep or making love in their beds. Like you could hear them chatting with friends as they wound up their long night at a party. You could almost sense those who were at work within. You could feel someone watching. Goosebumps rose on Megan's arms and she rubbed them away. She walked over and put the cover back over the canvas, breaking the spell in the room.

"Twenty grand! Now I really feel like dancing!" Megan exalted and shook her booty, making the other two women laugh.

The trio decided on stopping for pizza at the little shop that was just around the corner from the club. It was already filled with "vampires" and tattooed and pierced women and punks with large colorful Mohawks. They all looked ridiculously out of place and strangely beautiful under the fluorescent lights, scattered around little white Formica tables and crammed into worn orange pleather booths, eating pizza and French fries, trying not to smear their black lipstick. Megan wondered if she could somehow work it into a piece.

Megan ordered a large cheese while Gayle and Diane found a place for them to sit by the window. Diane was holding onto Gayle's hand like it was a lifeline keeping her from slipping in her heals on the checkerboard tiled floor. Megan hoped the poor thing would be able to eat with that thing on. She had laced her corset so tight you could see the indentations on her back. She looked hot, though, Megan admitted to herself magnanimously.

The girls ate and chatted idly about work and the couple told Megan about their new condo they had just closed escrow on and about how traffic would be terrible but how it was worth it to own rather than rent even if it meant moving to one of the satellite cities. They bought an upscale updated brownstone that had been divided into two townhouses. They went on and on about décor and contractors and tile selections. Megan listened intently as the couple shared their good fortune with her. She was glad the two successful women could afford their dream house in the coveted city of Arlington. It must have cost near a million and Megan couldn't wait to see it. Maybe she'd do a piece and give it to them as a house warming present.

After there were only a couple of slices left in the box and they all were stuffed to the point they didn't know how they'd walk out let alone dance. The girls vacated the table. Megan asked one of the spiked hair kids standing in the corner if they wanted the rest of the pizza and he said "cool" so they left it and walked out arm in arm in arm.

When they got in line in front of the club, Megan was glad she had switched bags for a much smaller one. She hated holding up lines so she could dig through the jumbled mess of her saddlebag to find things while people looked at her like "come on lady". She pulled her ID and admission money from the slim purse and handed it to the bouncer. After glancing at it and her face presumably to make sure it was her, he handed it back and she slid the card back in its pocket and let him stamp her hand. The words WELCOME TO HELL were there on the back of her wrist in black ink.

They checked their coats, handing the numbered tickets to Diane, as she was the most responsible, and the three headed straight to the ladies room downstairs to primp and reapply makeup.

At this club, there were two bathrooms. The men's room and the unisex bathroom which was the ladies room. This was so the straight guys could pee without worrying about having gay guys in the bathroom with them. Everyone else shared the unisex with the ladies and it made the men's room seem boring. Just a bathroom. Even some of the cooler straight guys realized that fact and braved the unisex.

The restroom was done all in dark purple and there was a huge gilt framed mirror above the sinks where most of the occupants were squished together in front of. Men and women were fixing makeup or messing it up making out. Queens were adjusting wigs and the words divine and fabulous was sprinkled liberally through the air. Not many people would know it but this room was the heart of the night club.

Satisfied that everyone looked fabulous and their bladders empty, they made their way back upstairs to the bar. The club had two large rooms and two DJs. The one with the bar was the better one. The music was hot and you could really dance to it. The other room was filled with the young emo kids and the music was a little whinier. Luckily for them, there were three stools open at the bar since it was early, and the ladies climbed up and called to the bartender who was dressed all in white with a glow stick around his neck, probably worn so you could spot him in the sea of black clothing. They ordered the special of the night which was called "The Devil's Tit" it was basically a Slippery Nipple with some grenadine added. It was too sweet for Megan's taste but they clinked their glasses together and Gayle said "bottoms up bitches" inciting giggles, and all three sipped their cocktails obligingly.

Megan didn't really drink much because of her mother so she was content to just nurse the small glass. She knew that Gayle would probably get drunk and rowdy and Diane would have to drag her home with fake promises of partying throughout the night. Diane probably had the same thought the moment Megan did because before the bartender came back to ask to refill

Gayle's glass and Diane had dragged her girlfriend off to the dance floor.

Immediately after the couple vacated their spots, a guy came and sat next to Megan.

"Hey, sexy. Can I buy you a drink?" he offered.

Megan shuddered a little. This guy was creepy. He was one of those thirty-something guys that worked a nine to five and had kids and a wife who he told he was working late while really he trolled the clubs like these to find women who he assumed would be into some kink. She could see the white line on his finger where his wedding band was supposed to be. Maybe he would even get to watch a couple of chicks make out. Gag. She hated this guy instantly. He stood out like a sore thumb in his Oscar de la Renta suit with a power tie tucked in his pocket.

"No thanks," Megan answered without even looking at him.

"It's just a drink, Babe," he pleaded.

He put a hand on her back and Megan felt like she had been touched by a snake.

"Fuck off!" she said loudly as she slid from the chair and went to stand next to the biggest guy in the room.

She looped her arm through his. Mr. Creepy seemed

to have gotten the message and looked to the next woman he planned on harassing.

"Thanks," Megan said and moved to walk away.

The big man laughed and grabbed her arm back. When he looked down at her Megan actually felt her knees weaken. This guy was gorgeous. He was an Adonis. She actually wanted to reach up and touch his face and probably would of if she wasn't frozen to the spot. Her mouth flooded with saliva. She thought she might drool with her mouth hanging open like that so she shut it with a clack that she hoped only she heard.

He smiled deeper and a dimple appeared in his smoothly shaven cheek as he asked, "What was all that about then?"

Megan's mouth seemed suddenly too dry to answer. "Sorry," she croaked out weakly and waved a hand at the suit at the bar. "Just trying to get out of dumping my drink on someone."

His laugh was like honey. Rich and deep and smooth. "Well, I'm glad I could come to your rescue then."

She hadn't noticed the slight lilt in his deep voice or that she hadn't taken her hand out of his big warm grasp.

"I thought you actually wanted to dance with me."

He managed to look hurt but he had the light of humor still on his beautiful face.

"I, uh." She faltered.

He was way too beautiful to be straight, Megan told herself. She looked lamely at her friends to come to her rescue as they danced to the slower rhythm of the song. They were completely wrapped up in each other and the music. She loved this song. It was one of her favorite bands. He didn't give her too long to protest and she didn't seem to have it in her power to do so. She let this stranger pull her onto the dance floor and wrap his strong arms around her waist. She rested her face on his muscled chest because it seemed like the right thing to do. *God, he smells good!* His scent was Bergamot and spice and leather and something else she wasn't sure of. She resisted the urge to bury her face in his chest and inhale him.

When the song ended Megan backed away reluctantly, feeling a little dizzy. She looked up past his muscled shoulder and saw her friends looking at her mouthing, "Who's that?" behind their hands while pointing discretely at him. She gave a slight shrug to let them know it was whatever and thanked him before walking over to her friends, face red.

Gayle was leaning down toward Diane and they were talking into each other's ears, probably about her from the smirks they were sending her way.

"So?" Gayle stared her down expectantly.

"So what?" Megan said, still stunned and warm from the dance.

"So who's the hunky guy you were drooling over on the dance floor?" Gayle looked her over not missing the blush on her cheeks even in the dim light.

"I wasn't drooling." Megan scoffed.

"Well?" Diane asked. "Who is he? Even Gayle thinks he's hot and she's a real snob."

"Shut up Di!" Gayle giggled.

"Look, I know how to appreciate beauty is all. Don't go getting all jealous on me now."

They were all teasing each other and some of the embarrassment faded and Megan relaxed her slim shoulders.

"He's still staring at you, you know," Diane informed her as she looked over her drooped shoulder. Megan turned completely red again. Her entire body felt like it was on fire.

"Don't stare!" She admonished her in a whisper.

Gayle grabbed her arm and pushed her toward the

empty red velvet couch ingeniously placed in an alcove in the corner of the room next to the bar. They walked in a line. Diane teetering a little until Gayle grabbed her arm and pulled her to her side. They sat on either side of her on the couch and began their questioning.

He could not figure out what just happened. He looked to the corner of the room to where the three women sat with their heads bent together in a huddle. In all his many years Gabriel had never been seen by anyone, *anyone* unless he expressly wanted them to see him. He hadn't, in his wildest dreams, expected to see *her* in the Stingray. It didn't dawn on him that he'd ever run into her anyplace though that was probably silly of him. Of course, a young woman could go about town whenever she chose.

He was still rocked by the sight of her up close. He had held her, danced with her even. He shook the hair off his shoulders. He had come to hunt. He certainly hadn't intended to make himself seen by anyone, especially by her. Or let her touch him. Or talk to him. Or to dance with her. What happened? Maybe when he saw that man touching her he had let his guard down. That had to be it. It was all too unexpected. Someone his age simply did not make mistakes. He was being as foolish as a schoolboy.

He looked down at his hands. He could still feel the warmth of her satiny skin against him. He could still smell her hair. He shook himself once more as if to shake off the feeling as an animal would shake away the rain and moved to lean against the bar and gather his thoughts. They circled through his mind and he found himself stealing glances at the space she occupied in the shadows.

What was it with this girl? He had been watching her for quite some time. He wasn't even sure why he continued doing so. He'd spend his nights out walking and could see the light in her window. It had seemed like she was the only one in the world awake besides him. He had gone closer to see what she was doing. What he saw from below was a beautiful woman standing completely nude in front of an easel, painting the darkness that was his haven, as if it held even more splendor and life than when the sun drenched it all in color. He had been awestruck not only by her but by unadorned beauty but by her incredible talent.

He had come to watch her more than a few times since then and no longer just because he was compelled to. It was always when the night was at its zenith, and always while she was completely consumed with her work. He hadn't intended to prey on her or stalk her. He just liked knowing that this beautiful creature shared his love of the night. He knew he didn't intend to hunt her. She didn't seem the type to be susceptible anyway. The real questions were why had he shown himself to her and what *were* his intentions? He didn't have an answer. He thought for a moment about melting back into the shadows and disappearing from sight but didn't know if the women were watching now and if they'd notice and remark on it. Risky or not he had to try. He needed to feed before going home to sort through his many questions. It was going to be a long night indeed.

Megan filled in her eager friends on the details of her encounter with the mystery guy and hero to the best of her ability, Megan risked a glance up to try to spot him. Maybe he'd be dancing with someone else by now. She tried not to let her disappointment show when she didn't see him in the room. She waved her friends off as they went to get more drinks and do some more dancing and used the opportunity to search without them teasing.

After a couple of disappointing trips to the bar and to

the bathroom without seeing him, Megan decided it was time to call it a night. She walked over to Gayle and Diane who were in a little circle of other women who must have been friends and told them she was going back to the apartment.

Diane asked, "Are you sure you don't want to wait for us to walk you back?"

"No, I'm good. This is my neighborhood, remember?"

Megan hugged both women and headed for the door almost forgetting to get her jacket. She fished in her little purse before remembering that Diane had the ticket for the coatroom.

She thought she saw the women heading to the bathroom so she walked down and pushed open the door. She could hear Gayle.

"…I just hate that she's so lonely. Even in college, she didn't have any boyfriends."

"Does she play for our team?" Diane asked.

"Di, if she did I'd know. Trust me. We lived together for five years. Never even a glance," she put a hand over her heart as she answered wistfully and they both laughed.

Megan wasn't sure when or even if she should butt in. She could feel her cheeks burning. It hurt her feelings to know that her friends were talking about her behind her back as if she was some pathetic recluse. So what if she didn't have time to date or that no one really caught her interest? That was her business. She was picky. She had every right to be. It was her goddamned body.

"Excuse me, honey," said a slender man in a studded dress.

"Sorry," Megan said, wiping a tear from beneath her eye. She pushed into the bathroom just as Gayle and Diane had turned to the door.

"I forgot my ticket," she said as if she hadn't heard half of their conversation.

Megan handed the little red ticket to the girl behind the counter. While she went to match up the tickets Megan gave one more look around disappointed. She had some fantasy in the back of her mind that the long haired hunk would appear next to her and offer to take her home. She shrugged her jacket on and walked out, denying the itch to look back just once more. Maybe she was lonely and desperate.

A middle-aged man rushed down the dark and empty
streets and ducked into an alley, looking behind him
nervously. He let out a sigh as the patrol car passed by
without slowing. He didn't notice the big man waiting
for him in the shadows until it was too late. The struggle
only lasted a moment before an odd calm came over him.
He allowed the larger figure to place his lips on his and
in a rush, his life and his crimes passed before his mind's
eye. Tears streamed down his acne scarred face and the
world went black.

CHAPTER 3

Megan did not sleep well. Only minutes after she got home from the club she received a text from Gayle asking if she made it home alright and saying they'd be spending the night at a friend's place they ran into and that they would pick the car up in the morning. That was fine with Megan. She was no longer in the mood for company.

She had peeled off the dress and shoes and threw them in front of the closet. She had planned on going straight to bed but as soon as she lay down she realized how impossible that was. She kept seeing *his* face. She got up in frustration at her sleeplessness.

She had paced a bit and opened her window to lean out. The air was nippy and her skin was already chilled from the walk and covered in goosebumps. She idly rubbed her arms and went to put on her old fashioned voluminous flannel nightgown. Normally she wouldn't bother but now she was grateful for its warmth. Its long white sleeves gathered with elastic at the wrists and left her hands unfettered and snug enough to go back to her post. She stared into the night. Her eyes touching on familiar houses and familiar views. Some dwellings with their lights still on while other windows were darkened, their inhabitants long-gone to bed or still enjoying the night safely indoors. The streets desolate except for a stray police car or those up to no good for whom they kept their vigil.

She felt comforted and possessive. This was *her* view. Her houses. Her city. Her night.

After sitting so long on the sill staring at the rooftops, Megan's muscles had begun to stiffen. She reluctantly relinquished her cherished perch and got up to stretch. She walked over to her newly finished painting. She stared at it again with renewed awe. She really had captured the night in that one. She even imagined that the man on the church was the man she danced with at the club. Maybe he sat up there on that church, watching the world bathed in twilight, as she did. The thought made her feel less alone.

Gabe looked down at the darkened cityscape. He had a lot to think about. The desire to hunt had finally waned after the encounter with his beautiful artist.

Yes, he had begun to think of her as his. That was just one more thing for him to ponder. He was home. Well, the place he now resided. He felt like he hadn't spent a night there in weeks and in truth he hadn't much.

His gaze went out once more until sharpening on the window he knew so well. Of course, the light was on in the studio. Was she painting? Was she thinking about their meeting as he was or did she forget the whole thing? Did she still feel her heat as he felt hers? He wasn't sure why but he hoped so.

He was tempted to go over and see what she was doing but he was unsure now of his ability to remain unseen by her. He had no clue what to do about *that* so he put the thought aside for later. He felt like he *had* to see her again but it wasn't like he could just happen to meet her again on the street in broad daylight and ask her to coffee but there had to be some way to deal with his curiosity of the girl. Especially now that she had seen him. And he had held her.

Would've he have fed on her if it was possible? he mused. *No*, she wasn't for that. *What was she for?* It wasn't like he just hung around people for pleasure. He hadn't had any real interest in the world at all in many years besides work. Until her. She seemed to draw him to her like a compass to true north. He wiped a hand across his face. His addiction to her was growing stronger. He had to figure it all out so he could go back to the peace of just being.

With sleep an impossibility, Megan decided she may as well be productive. She prepared *Nightwatch* for the gallery. That's what she'd named the painting. She wrapped it carefully in brown paper and banded it with twine and attached the computer printout with all the pertinent information to the front. With that out of the way she grabbed a vanilla coke from the fridge and unwrapped a cherry Pop-tart and got out her sketchbook and charcoals.

She knew she had intended to sketch him. It had seemed like everything else was some slow dance leading up to the task. She just couldn't help herself any longer.

She took the blanket off the couch and headed back over to the window seat. The white paper gleamed in the wash of moonlight as she touched the soft coal to the pad. His face came to life with sure, loving strokes. His long, thick hair that curled like mahogany to his shoulders. His devilish smile, his sweet dimple on his right cheek. She smudged here and there making the hollows of his cheeks and his high cheekbones. She made his strong brow and his chin soft and slightly creased. She traced the graceful arches of his brows and his glittering grey eyes. They looked like an ocean after a storm.

Here on paper, he looked exactly as he did when he was staring down at her from the dance floor at the club. Megan looked at his lips that she had drawn. Soft and full and smiling and felt weak all over again. She ran a finger carefully over them without smudging the coal. She felt a tingling between her legs and her breasts ached, her nipples already hardened from the cold night air, and felt the storm she saw in his eyes now coursing through her body.

She put the pad down on the sill and stared for a while at the likeness. Megan wondered where the handsome stranger was now. No, not a stranger. She felt she recognized him on some other deep, hidden level. Her body knew him. She felt it, like a lost memory teasing the surface but never rising fully.

She remembered how he had looked at her. His mischievous smile on his perfectly bowed lips.

How would they feel on her own? she wondered. *How would he taste?*

She tried to picture his large, well-muscled body. How he looked in the clinging leather pants with his shirt unbuttoned, showing and expanse of well-toned pecs sprinkled with soft dark hair. Megan tried to recapture in her mind the smell and feel of him pressed against her body. So familiar and so perfect. The way her head fit just in the hollow of his chest as though it was meant to.

Her nipples tightened almost painfully as she soaked herself in memories of him, adding to them her own fantasies. She reimagined the scene on the dance floor but in her thoughts, the scene had changed and he was leaning down to kiss her as they swayed to the music. She could feel the cool breeze wafting in on them as they danced right there in front of her window instead of in the crowded club. There was only him. His warm mouth and teasing tongue wreaking havoc on her senses. He nuzzled the hollow of her neck and licked his way down to her shoulder. The feminine curves of her soft body pressed along the length of his hardened one and the fitted leather pants he wore felt like bare flesh to the touch.

Megan let the scene unfold on its own. She pictured him lifting her in his corded arms and placing gently on the mattress before climbing on her bed with her. His beautiful athletic body draped across the big four-poster as she explored every inch of his physique with her hands as if she were sculpting him herself. She could feel the slightly roughened skin of his palms as he molded and kneaded her curves, making her moan with delight. Her nightgown seemed to melt away at his touch. She felt him sliding his hands over her body in a frenzy as he rocked against her while she straddled him. He bent his head to suckle a breast, teasing the other sensitized tip of the opposite one with his skilled fingers every so often flicking his tongue from one to the other. Making sure each was equally and exquisitely loved.

She envisioned him standing by the bed and slowly peeling off his leather pants. She took a moment to admire the perfection of his form before he knelt on the bed before her. He was more beautiful than any statue of any Greek god she had ever seen.

He put his hands on her knees and parted her legs and admired her in a way that made her feel beautiful and desired, before dipping his head down to taste her. His hair was like silk on her belly and his tongue was like fire, licking flames through her swollen flesh up through her womb and out her breasts. When she was writhing beneath his kiss and thought she couldn't take even one more flick of his tongue, he gracefully slid up her quivering body and, laying between her spread thighs, looked straight into her eyes and into her soul. He bent his beautiful face toward hers again and brushed kisses over her pouting, panting lips. Her body quaked with anticipation as he, poised above her, rubbed the thick head of his shaft over her moist bud, over and over, making her cry out, before sliding it into her slick opening in one powerful thrust that shattered both her innocence and the room around her into a million shimmering pieces.

Megan gasped, her orgasm ripping through her. Colors swirled and pulsed around and through her until she floated back to earth. He pumped into her furiously until he roared his own release as she arched and climaxed savagely against him once more before he collapsed on the bed beside her.

She didn't remember falling asleep with his name unspoken on her lips.

Gabriel couldn't remember the last time he had dreamed. He was roused from his bed because he thought he heard Megan calling out his name. He was nude and every inch of him was rock hard although he hadn't remembered taking off his clothing. *What a dream*, he thought. It had to be one. His imagination running wild. If he hadn't known exactly where he was, on the second floor of the old church he had converted into his home, he would swear he was in Megan's bed. *It was only a dream* he told himself again. He had not gone over to her apartment. The fact that it began *before* he went to sleep was easily explainable if he bothered to try he was sure.

He had been sitting at his usual perch, statue still, letting his thoughts war through him. He had been staring into her window. That much he could remember. He had been honed in on her building, fighting the urge to go and see her. The temptation was almost unbearable so he went to lie down in the darkness of his bed and listen to the night. He remembered lying there quietly before being sucked into what could only be a fantasy. He had been thinking about her so hard he had actually felt like he was with her. Making love to her. In her bed. He could swear he smelled her dark scent on his skin still.

His body grew hard as he remembered the taste of her. Gabe groaned. He had forgotten how powerfully real dreams or even fantasies could be. So long he couldn't actually remember even having them. He would enjoy every bit of the rarity while it was fresh in his mind. He lay back on the pillow and allowed himself to relive the erotic reverie as he drifted back into oblivion.

She woke up early, her body draped across her bed awkwardly. She was sore and half frozen. She shut the window and unfolded her stiff body and walked over to the coffeemaker and made a pot, then to the bathroom where she turned the tap on high to set a bath. She poured jasmine and vanilla scented bubbles into the hot water and left it to fill.

She stretched her cramped body in the kitchen and poured a steaming cup of the fragrant brew and made her way back to the bathroom. She shut the faucet and got in, coffee mug still in hand, and sank down into the bubbles up to her chin. The warm water melted the stiffness and cold from her body and she sighed, taking sips from the rim of the smooth porcelain that she held just above the surface of the bath.

Her thoughts drifted back to the night before and to him. Her nipples hardened to peaks and she flushed at just the thought of him. She had gone to sleep dreaming of making love to him and now her body remembered it as though it really happened. Her pelvis was sore and there was a small rust stain on the sheets that she had noticed when she slid out of them. Maybe her period was starting early, she thought.

Megan was already out of the tub and dressed when Billy came by with his truck a little after twelve. Diane had gone and picked up the car sometime earlier without stopping in but Gayle had called from her office to tell her and to let her know that the painting was being picked up before one.

Megan let the lanky kid in and offered him some coffee and one of the donuts that she picked up shortly before. Bill said no to the coffee but grabbed one of the glazed donuts and after jerking his head to get a hank of dirty brown hair out of his eyes, shoved it in his mouth in one bite.

The boy was the epitome of gangly. He was about six feet tall and only one hundred or so pounds. He wore ridiculously tight jeans that looked like they were a second skin and were covered with rips and paint splats.

He finished the look with a brown flannel shirt with a grimy red bandana tied around his arm. Megan knew he was an art student doing an internship at the gallery so she asked him about his work. They sat at the little table and talked about new art exhibits and up and coming artists and whose work sucked. The last was discussed at length and with delight.

After Billy had polished off five out of the six donuts in the box he got up to get back to work. She wondered to herself how someone could be so painfully thin and eat like that, suddenly self-conscious of her rounded thighs and big bottom as she at the remaining jelly.

Megan helped the thin youth heft the large canvas after he had put it in the crate and wrapped it, and they both carried it carefully down the stairs and laid it face-up in the back of the pickup.

"Thanks for the donuts Meg," Billy waved bye as he hopped in the driver's seat and started the engine.

Megan always liked Billy. He was a good kid. He even let her slide him a tip. He stuffed the twenty bucks in his pocket and blushed out a thank you. She waved at the moving GMC and smiled.

Gayle called again less than an hour later to talk

business.

"Megan darrr-ling," she cooed in her "let's discuss numbers" voice, "I love *Nightwatch* and I really can get you the twenty grand for it but listen, hon," she paused, not a good sign and Megan wondered what the inevitable catch, "I really think this should be a series. The last two you gave me sold within the week," Megan knew exactly where this was going, "I want five more pieces at least and you are going to have a proper showing."

That was it. It was an order, not a request. *Nightwatch* was now a hostage along with the money that she'd receive for it. Gayle knew that Megan hated the glitzy gallery showings and had up until that moment been very understanding. They had discussed the topic vehemently and regularly with neither agreeing with the other and both requiring a time out afterward. Now her friend was finally going to force her hand. She should have known that the twenty g's was merely the carrot being dangled by the savvy blonde.

Gayle had said that showings were a must for selling paintings at that price. The buyers wanted to meet the artist. Examine their work. Feel like they were in the limelight when they bought a piece, like they were part of the art community. A part of the art, etc.

Megan just wished they would buy them because they liked them and leave it at that and expressed as much. She didn't like the schmoozing and the gaudiness of art society events.

"When do you want them by BOSS?"

She felt a little guilty for the barb. Gayle wasn't being mean, she had been a lot more patient with Megan because of their relationship and they both knew it.

Megan asked the question with all of the disappointment she felt apparent in her tone. She knew it was unfair to ask Gayle for any more favors. It was time to be a grown up. If she wanted to call herself a "real" artist she had to do the dirty work too. She didn't have to like it, though.

"Next month," Gayle sounded resolved and cool, "We're having a gala in October. Tourist season."

Gayle knew Megan long enough to know her feelings on the subject and also that her friend knew that she'd do it if she was pushed.

Gayle hated to use both her friendship and her power to get Megan to do this but it had to be done. Her best friend had real talent. It was a shame for it to go to waste. Her art should be shared with the world and would be if Gayle had a say. Those showcase jitters should have gone away after college and probably would have if Gayle hadn't been the one selling Megan's pieces. She was a class-A enabler. She owed this to her.

"I'll have Cassie call you with the details."

She was definitely using her boss-lady voice although her tone softened just a bit, "This will be good for you Megan," she added into the silence, sounding less and less like the dragon lady she had affected moments before.

"Gee. Well then thanks, *mom*," she laughed.

Megan tried to sound angry but she wasn't really. Not anymore. No one knew better than her best friend that she was just scared. She was afraid she'd drop the ball and disappoint everyone. Megan didn't work very well with deadlines and was never comfortable showing her work to *anyone* let alone the Haute Monde. She always felt like it wouldn't be good enough and everyone would see she was a wannabe. A fake. Plus she hated people looking at her. It made her feel self-conscious and awkward.

"Sorry. Didn't sleep well. You know I can be a cranky bitch," she mumbled finally, feeling sorry for being such an ungrateful brat in the face of what was a wonderful opportunity that any sane artist would kill for.

"I know, Honey. Drink more coffee," Gayle said sympathetically.

"So, what the heck time did you guys wrap it up last night?" Megan changed the subject so her friend would know she wasn't holding any grudges.

"Oh my God! You should've seen Di trying to help me up the stairs in those heels!" she dove in, laughing heartily, sounding more like the twenty-five year old Gayle who Megan loved. The one who delighted in the dramatic and the absurd, "Needless to say we both took a tumble and I owe her a night at The Palm in a pantsuit."

Megan shuddered audibly at the mention of a pantsuit and just like that the friends had steered the conversation easily back to neutral territory.

CHAPTER 4

Megan stood in front of The Blarney Stone staring at a spot of paint on her boot. She knew she would have to walk up to the heavy wooden double doors and enter the dimly lit pub in a moment. Her mother would no doubt call her if she was even a minute late. She just wasn't ready to face Josephine and whatever draining request she would make on her daughter just yet. She needed a few more deep breaths. She would not tell her about the show just yet, if ever. She didn't need any more blows to her fragile self-esteem or any questions asked that would only worsen her nerves.

The cement sidewalk in front of the pub was freshly swept and the large black iron urns of pansies that stood at either side of the entryway had been cleared of cigarette butts from the night before. Megan could hear the soft sounds of Irish folk music as it escaped through the door that was left slightly ajar. The lunch crowd would be long gone and only employees and a handful of dedicated drinkers would be scattered around the gleaming bar and scarred wooden tables.

Her time to stall had run out. One of the big black doors flung open and Hamish Calhoun stood, filling every inch of the massive door frame. He was loudly finishing a conversation over a shoulder to someone inside. He reached in his black trousers and produced a pack of Marlborough reds and a shiny silver lighter with a Red Sox logo on the front. He turned to cup one hand in front of the flame to light up when he saw Megan standing there.

"Megs my girl!" he boomed, a huge smile splitting his big red face. He took a deep drag from the cigarette between his lips before pulling it out and making a gesture with his hands, "Your ma said you might be comin' ta see the likes of us."

He put the cigarette back in his mouth and stretched out his arms that resembled oak trees, waiting for an embrace. Megan stepped up to the colossal man and let him enfold her in a bear hug. He smelled like he always did. Like booze and sweat mixed with fried potatoes and tobacco. He smelled like home.

"Hey, Uncle Ham!"

She stepped back to take a good look at him. He only looked a slightly older than the last time she saw him. There was a little more white in his orange hair and a few more creases in his ruddy skin, especially around his jewel blue eyes. This only made him look more formidable, though.

Megan always wanted to sketch Uncle Ham in a kilt with a broadsword in his hand. It seemed fitting for his look. He'd be and interesting subject. Megan remembered when she was little she thought they called him Ham because his fist was as big and as pink as one.

She beamed up at him affectionately before leaning in once more and anxiously asking, "How is she?"

Hamish looked down at her sharply.

"Go in and see for yourself," he grumbled, "she hasn't had more than one drink a night in weeks."

Uncle Ham's face showed signs of weariness and infinite patience. This was surprising news and he gave her a minute to digest the information. Megan watched him watching her as she chewed over his words. It wasn't that her mother hadn't quit drinking a few times, usually after a long period of being really terrible for a while then hitting rock bottom. Or she would just outright lie about her sobriety as a means of manipulating her daughter. Megan decided this news wasn't said to illicit a reaction and may not be far from the truth if simply for the strain on the big man's face at the admission or sheer the novelty of the older woman not quitting outright but cutting down. It was typically all or nothing with Josephine Black.

Usually, Josephine would only swear she quit cold turkey as a way to sway Megan into becoming a part of her life again and the two or so days it lasted would be pure hell on everyone. Dealing with Josephine while she detoxed was an experience not for the timid. She'd careen back and forth between overcompensating as a mother and treating her like she was twelve, making sandwiches with the crusts cut off and taking her shopping, to angrily accusing Megan of being an ungrateful chit who thought she was too good to be around her poor immigrant mother. Cutting down to one drink, though, she had never tried that one before and Megan wondered what that would be like. Newness scared her, especially when it involved her mother.

Emotions warred in Megan's head as she tried to assess the foreign situation. She had always tried to adjust herself to whatever mood her mother was in. Less drama that way. She knew that if she said one wrong thing, Josephine would begin the tirade that would whittle her down and make her feel like the helpless child she once was.

Ham just continued to watch Megan's face intently until she seemed to have worked it out. No one understood the complicated relationship between mother and daughter like Uncle Ham.

Megan and her mother had lived above The Blarney Stone for most of Megan's life. Josephine sang there regularly and waited tables and did the cleaning to pay the rent.

Hamish hadn't owned the bar very long before he and Josie met. Before being the proprietor of the authentic Irish pub, he had been both a boxer and a nightclub bouncer. He had often said that hiring Josie was the smartest thing he'd ever done and that he owed all the Blarney Stone's business success to her. Megan had known that Uncle Ham was probably just being kind by not acknowledging the truth which was obvious. He took in Josie and her all those years back because he pitied them and they had no place else to go and because he needed someone with an Irish accent to make it authentic.

Megan wasn't sure if Ham and her mother were

lovers but she was always sure he was completely in love with Josephine. You could see it in his twinkling blue eyes every time he looked at her. Yes, there was love there even when it was masked by a sadness that she had never been able to put a finger on.

Ham was like a father to her in so many ways. He had taken care of her and her mother throughout her childhood. Making sure she was fed. Giving her rides to school. Protecting her from her mother when she had too much to drink. Taking her to the hospital when she needed her appendix out and to the dentist when she had a cavity. Uncle Ham had been her rock. She felt bad she had let her relationship with her mother stop her from visiting him more often. He was the closest thing to a father that she ever had. Hell, closest thing to any kind of parent, she thought, letter her thoughts turn bitter once more.

Megan reached up and patted the older man's closely shaven cheek. His eyes glittered for a second at the familiar gesture.

"Be a good girl Megs," he said and he put a hand on her back and gave her a little shove through the open door.

Josephine was perched at the long and lustrous oak bar watching the doorway as if expecting her, the glasses and bottles were backlit and their gleam cast her in an ethereal hue that brought out her beauty.

When her daughter entered, the older woman straightened and stared at the glass of Coke in front of her as if that was what had her interest the whole time. She was not the type to get up and go to her daughter and give her a hug or to wave and bubble like an idiot at her own child. Instead, she looked up hesitantly. Almost shyly although she was a proud woman that no one would ever make the mistake of calling shy. Stubborn and calculating was more like it. Josie Black would not make the first move. She waited for Megan to come and take a seat beside her dutifully. She looked at her as if looking at the person walking toward her, the woman with her own face, was a stranger and in so many ways she was. That's probably as it should be. She had never understood the girl just as her own mother had never understood her.

Thinking of her mother triggered an automatic response and when her glass touched her lips, Josie was disappointed to find it only contained soda. She had forgotten.

Megan sidled up to her mother on the closest barstool, putting her big purse on the one next to her.

"Hi Ma," she said casually.

The truth was she hadn't seen her mother in almost two months. Not since the Fourth of July cookout and now she found the distance had made her both cautious and curious. What could make Josephine Black stop drinking this time? She was expecting that her mom going to tell her she was sick or something. Or had been going to church. Both had happened a few times in the past but not long enough to have any lasting effects on the older woman. She loved her whiskey and with that love came the inevitable heartaches and so the vicious cycle continued.

Her mother, instead of speaking, slid an opened manila envelope in front of her. Curious, Megan looked at the address in the corner. It was from a lawyer's office in Galway. She looked at her mother quizzically,

"What's this?" she asked.

She didn't get an answer and Josephine hadn't even bothered to look up from her glass which Megan was relieved to find was non-alcoholic, so she pulled the sheaf of papers out of the envelope with shaking hands. At first blush, she assumed the papers had something to do with her grandparents. Maybe they had died, she guessed. She had never met them before and her mother never spoke of them really so she felt no real kinship or sadness at the supposed loss. She wasn't even sure if they were very old or not.

Megan wondered if her mother had spoken to them at all since she left them and Ireland behind at the age of nineteen.

Josephine pulled into herself even further as her only child looked from the envelope to her face but she remained blank, not giving anything away.

She had, in truth, thought along the same lines when she had seen address on the envelope when it had arrived three weeks before. She had received such a letter when her father had passed and thought maybe this one was about her mother. She had left the packet unopened for almost a week, drinking heavily to dull the pain and anger that throbbed in her heart at seeing something from home. The terrible pain and regret she felt when she thought of her parents were all too familiar and so was her means of dulling it.

The small suburb of Dun Donald where her parents presumably resided still was no longer home. Her folks were average poor Irish. Meaning they were Catholics with a lot of children living in the north, her Da drank heavily and worked long shifts, and her Ma was always angry and tired but sometimes she missed them all dearly.

Megan had extracted the sheaf of papers from the envelope. Her mother still had not spoken a word. She seemed wrapped up in some inner turmoil and kept looking at the tumbler of soda ruefully.

"I don't understand," Megan said finally after reading through the papers for the most part. The documents inside were addressed to her.

The first one read:

For the Eyes of Megan Black,

I am sorry to inform you of your father's passing on August 28 of this year. The funeral arrangements were made and carried out according to his final wishes that he had also set forth in his will. Regrettably, I could not send you adequate notice of the observances owing to trying to locate your address. Contained herein are two plane tickets and other information regarding arrangements made for your accommodations while staying in Ireland for the reading of your father's will. You, being sole heir to the Estate of the late Jonathan Lucas Donavan must attend the reading and dispense your father's property per his last wishes.

I look forward to meeting you here. Please make sure you read all of the information enclosed so you will know what is necessary for your trip.

Sincerest Condolences,
Peter McCredie Esq.

"I think they've made some kind of mistake Ma." Megan was so confused. She handed her mother the letter, "They must have gotten the wrong Megan Black.

Josephine looked at her sharply. She looked so much older all of a sudden.

"No, honey," she said, "It's not a mistake."

When confronted with questions about her father during Megan's youth, Josephine had told her daughter lies. As far as Megan was concerned, her father's name was Luke Shannahan. He and her mother had met in Ireland and were childhood sweethearts. They had intended to get married when he died in a fishing accident. Josephine, in her sadness had left her home so as not to be reminded of the tragedy.

Seemingly out of nowhere, Ham brought over two coffee cups and saucers and set them down on the bar.

"Coffee, ya?" he asked. Megan nodded and tried to smile at the older man, "Brilliant!" he said and poured the steaming liquid into the cup and placed a caddy with creamers and sugar packets from behind the bar onto the wood beside it. "I'll bring you a wee bit of a tuck," he said and left the ladies once more to talk and headed into the kitchen.

Josephine needed to explain to Megan the real story. It was so painful and shameful that she just wanted a drink. Her mouth had gone dry and the coffee wasn't helping. She had to release this awfulness on her child. Let her know she wasn't ever loved or wanted by her own father. Josephine knew what that pain all too well and had tried to spare her. She had to tell her she lied and why.

Ham knew the whole story and he had told her countless times to tell her daughter before she had gone off to college but Josephine didn't want her to be distracted when she should have been studying or at least that what she told Ham. The truth was she wasn't sure if her daughter would ever speak to her again once she knew the shame of her own origins and her part in it. She also didn't want Megan to dwell on the stigma of being the abandoned bastard child of a deadbeat father who was a passing fling of her loose mother who at the time of her conception, didn't even know his last name.

Josephine had left the all-girls high school in Leenaun at seventeen and worked at the local pub serving food and drink to the workers after their shifts. On weekends she played her acoustic guitar and sang folksongs for the tourists and townies alike in Galway. Her mother didn't approve but didn't stop her daughter either. As long as she still sang in the choir on Sundays and turned over her pay at the end of the week, the older woman would turn a blind eye to where her daughter went and what she was up to. She had six other children to worry about.

One night Josephine was playing in a small hole-in-the-wall pub in what used to be known as The Dun Lady. The house was packed but it was early enough that it hadn't gotten rowdy yet. She had just finished playing a set and had sat down at a table with an ale. The band would take over from that point on and she was content to stay as long as she may, not wanting to return to the overcrowded heat of her house and the coldness of her parents.

Not long after sitting down at one of the scarred round tables and propping her guitar case on the chair beside her, swinging her legs onto the seat with it, a man appeared at her side.

"You have a beautiful voice," he had said near her left ear.

"Thank ya. I'm here every week," she responded absently.

"Then I'll have to come here every week," he flirted.

Something in his tone piqued her curiosity and the redhead looked to him for the first time, into the most handsome face she had ever seen. She couldn't remember noticing him in the crowd but that was nothing unusual since she had barely paid attention to those who watched her through the haze of cigarette smoke that filled the small building but she was certain that she would've taken notice of a man like that. He was tall and striking with the most unusual emerald green eyes, shaded with thick lashes and thick wavy hair the color of walnuts that looked charmingly overdue for a haircut.

She blushed from head to toe when she realized she had been gawking at this stranger. She knew the red would be apparent with her fair coloring and she flushed deeper at that knowledge but managed another smaller, "Thanks."

He was smiling at her. One of his front teeth was a little crooked. It just made him look all the more charming.

"Mind if I sit?" he asked.

Josephine was not ugly by any means and was used to having all types of men ask her out, especially with Guinness as a social lubricant, but no one was as handsome as this man nor did they have his manners or his sense of ease and grace. His accent flagged him as an American. Most Americans she had met thus far were either rude or belligerently inebriated from trying to outdrink the locals. She moved the guitar and her feet. The gesture clearly telling him to do as he may. She clutched the cool glass in her hand, willing herself to sit still. She was not good at flirtation. Every thought she had showed clearly on her face. It was one of the downfalls of being a ginger and she hoped she wouldn't blunder too badly or her attraction to him to come off as so apparent it bordered on desperate.

He sat watching the thoughts flit across her beautiful face. She seemed nervous of him which he found amusing.

"Do you really play here a lot then?" he asked.

"Mmmph. I dunno what a lot is but I have played here before, I have. They just offered me a once a week gig and I play anywhere else that'll have me, I guess, so long as the drive home is not too long, mind," this was all let one in one long fast breath. She knew she was babbling and stopped short.

He smiled again. She looked embarrassed but it was hard for him to tell. She had turned scarlet the minute he came over and hadn't changed back yet to the peaches and cream complexion that had softly glowed as she sang. He loved the sultry huskiness of her voice though so he was determined to get her to relax and speak to him as much as possible.

A few drinks later she was definitely more at ease and they were speaking with no trouble. The blush had faded to the light pink flush of someone in their cups. She had told him all about her home and her music and her hopes of being discovered as a famous singer and songwriter like Carly Simon or Janis Joplin or the like.

"You certainly have the voice and the presence for it," he said sincerely and she beamed at his confidence in her abilities.

He didn't strike her as a flatterer or liar. He had

spoken little of himself. He had said he had gone to B.U. and that he traveled a lot, mostly doing charity work during the summers and during the study abroad program he was a part of.

Josephine had so many questions about all the places he had been. She had spoken passionately about traveling the world as much as he had, playing for fans throughout the globe. Her face had gone dreamy as he spoke of Paris and Rome although he had also mentioned traveling to India and studying a whole semester in England before spending his summer in Scotland only the year prior.

"So are you here for school then?" she asked him, entranced.

"Actually I just graduated last month and decided to take the summer off before settling into my career. I wanted to travel while I could before being too tied down with work. My grandfather was originally from Ardrahan before he emigrated. I thought it would be cool to explore my roots before I planted down my own. Ireland's an awesome place. Unlike anywhere else I've ever been. It has beauty takes my breath away," the last part was said huskily as if it were aimed directly toward her and not her homeland at all.

Josie's face flamed to match her hair once more.

The music had long since stopped playing and the pub had nearly cleared off of everyone save the band, a few employees and them. The manager came over and handed her an envelope with her night's pay. This was her cue to look at her watch. It was almost three in the morning and she had an hour drive home. She had to go before she got home to meet her Da as he was leaving for work. That would be a catastrophe.

Like a gentleman, he walked her out to her beat up red car, carrying her guitar over his shoulder. She leaned against the driver's side door and looked up at him with a coy smile while he shoved the case through the rear window into the back seat as she directed.

"It's been lovely," she said and looked through her lashes.

He took a step toward her and put his hands on her waist. He was about to bend down to kiss her but she held up a hand to his chest to stop him.

He was about to step back, disappointed when she asked, "What's your name?"

He hesitated before telling her.

"Luke," he said and she stood on tiptoe, capturing his lips for a deep kiss.

"Pleased ta meet ya, Luke," she said and got into her

car and drove off.

They spent the better part of the summer together, meeting up in her free time. They talked and she took him sightseeing but mostly spent their time making love in the little house he rented in the country.

Josephine, at age eighteen was completely and surely in love.

The young lovers spoke about the future but the stuff far off in the distance. They never discussed the immediate time ahead though, like why how long he'd be in Ireland or where he'd be going when he left. She knew his passions but not his job that he eluded to vaguely.

They lived those months in the stolen afternoons or evenings, discovering each other's youthful bodies and talking in dreams. They were all passion and no prudence. In hindsight, it was foolish of her to live in the moment like that. One day he was just gone. The rental empty.

Josephine had gone back to all the places they had been together, including the pub where they met. After two weeks of searching and asking around she was only certain of two things. One, was that he was gone and the last was that she was pregnant.

Josephine had spent the weeks following saving whatever money she could put by without her mum noticing. She was sick not only in body but in spirit too. It was becoming harder and harder to hide the mound of her belly from her parents or the fact that she was slipping out for air so that she could have privacy while losing her breakfast behind her mum's prized rose bushes. She was afraid of taking a shower and having one of her younger siblings burst in and discover her secret. She lived in abject terror every day.

She knew she had to tell her parents the truth of what was going on and when she did it was exactly as she expected. They threw her out.

"Ma. Da. I've got something to tell you both," she said at the table one Sunday morning after church while her younger brothers were outside playing cricket.

She knew getting them alone and away from impressionable young ears would be difficult on any other day.

"What is it Josephine?" her mother asked curiously.

"I'm pregnant."

She said it. Out loud. It felt flat and quiet. She sucked in a breath and tried not to throw up on the plate of eggs before her.

Her father had risen from his seat and turned and ugly purple. The newspaper he had been holding was rolled up in his enormous fist.

"Hold on Joe," her mother said, stilling him with her upraised palm for a moment, "Josie is a good girl and I'm just sure she is just havin' a bit o' trouble tellin' us that she eloped and married off with some Shaughnessy boy or something, now aren't ya Josie?" she prompted, "You're afraid you're Da and I won't give our blessing on the match?" her mother asked, trepidatiously, her eyes pleading.

Josephine hung her head. She wished she could assure her mother that that was the case. She mentally prepared for both the verbal and physical beating she was sure was going to follow her response. She covered her belly with both hands and didn't look up at them.

"There's no weddin' Mum. There's no goin' ta be a weddin."

"What do you mean there's no goin' ta be a weddin'?" her father bellowed.

"Maybe the lad's dead, Joe," her mother interjected hopefully.

They both looked at her eager that this was at least the case. She'd have to disappoint again.

"There is no lad Da," Josie shook her head sadly, "There'll be no weddin'. He went back ta America," she said with grim finality.

Joseph Black began hitting his only daughter about the head and neck with the folded up newspaper furiously. In between whacks he'd say things like, "My daughter's a whore!" and, "The devil take ya lass!" and, "There's no going ta be a weddin'!" and, "American bastard!"

At some point the beating had stopped and her mother had managed to put herself between her daughter and her irate husband. For a moment she thought her mum would defend her or tell her she loved her anyway but she was sorely disappointed.

"You're on your own now Josephine. Ya made your bed and now ya must lie in it. Your father and I are good Christian people and canna be associated with a loose, unrepentant daughter. What kind of an impression would that be on the little ones?" she didn't soften at all although there was a deep weariness etched in the slump of her shoulders and the lines beneath her eyes, "Ya have ten minutes to gather up your belongings and leave this house, Josephine. You're on your own now. God go with ya daughter."

She still hear her Da ranting as she packed, "No daughter of mine. My daughter's dead. Ya hear that lass? You're dead ta me!" on her way down the hall.

With no further words spoken between her and her family and only a wave given to her brothers, Josephine put the two duffel bags and guitar case into the backseat and drove away from the only home she'd ever known without looking back.

When she was out of sight she let the tears choke her and she pulled over and let the crushing grief consume her.

Josephine had, alone and pregnant, made her way through Ireland playing and singing for money until she had enough for a one way ticket to the States. No more was the plan to go across the pond to be a famous singer. No. Now she was going there on a different mission. She was going to find the bastard Luke and make him marry her.

Tears were streaking their way down Megan's cheeks as her mother regaled her with the heartbreaking story of how she came to be born.

She and her Ma had never been overly affectionate

but when Josephine had finished the story with being unable to find the man who'd gotten her pregnant after traveling to a foreign country alone and broke, and how she had to sing for her supper and wait tables right until she went into labor in the very pub they were sitting in, Megan leaned over and grasped her mother in a tight hug. All of the despair and guilt seemed to flow out of Josephine and bathed Megan in her grief, making her weep for the both of them. She had never understood this woman in her arms. Never knew the truth. It all made sense now. The drinking. The steering her away from boys and later, men. The love-hate relationship they had. All of it.

Megan felt like a horrible person for thinking her mother was selfish and uncaring. She had failed to show this woman who had been through so much to bring her into the world any shred of sympathy. She had been a selfish child. No more, she vowed to herself. Josephine may have a problem but Megan would no longer contribute to it by holding grudges and being mean.

They were both shaking like leaves as they pulled back from one another. Both tried to smile as they pulled themselves together a little. It should've been awkward but it wasn't. It was comforting. The distance between the two women no longer seemed insurmountable as each patted their hair and blotted away tear tracks.

Hamish Calhoun was a smart man. He took the moment when the two women, the apples of his eyes, were straightening themselves out after their embrace to bring out plates of corned beef sandwiches, fried pickles and crisps. Yes, Ham was smart enough to know that the remoteness would easily pool back between the women he loved if he did not find a way to cement the relationship for them. To be the glue. It was too sensitive of a time and he knew that if Josie gave Meg enough time to herself, she'd work her mind back around to being angry and confused over all the lies and possibly shut Josie out for good and him with her.

"Thanks, Uncle Ham," Megan said as she noticed the plate in front of her.

She started picking at the fries and pickles immediately. Ham pulled up his stool on the other side of the bar and put his own matching plate on the brass rails and dug right in as well.

"Eat sometin', for Christ sakes Josie," he said through a mouthful of sandwich.

Josie crinkled her delicate nose at him and shot him a death stare but pulled her own plate in front of her and bit into a fry pointedly.

"Good lass," Ham said with a satisfied smile, "Now Megs, tell your Uncle Ham what you've been workin' on," he demanded in his light brogue and shot Josie a covert wink.

Ham had cleared the plates and ducked back in the kitchen after they'd finished lunch.

"So are ya goin' then?" Josephine nodded her head at the envelope.

"Will you come with me?" Megan asked, unsure.

This was new territory for her. She wasn't afraid of travel, not in the least. Megan just needed someone who knew this stranger, her father, to be there with her to deal with the business of his death. She wasn't equipped at all for this, she thought. The only feeling for this man was anger and she wasn't sure that was an appropriate feeling to have in light the circumstances. It seemed inappropriate that she wouldn't be mourning.

"I'll tink about it Meg," her mother said, but she was sure from the look of the other woman, she'd rather dive headfirst into the mouth of a volcano.

CHAPTER 5

Megan stopped at the little grocery store and picked up some fruit and milk and Oreos then realized she was still starved and caved and went to the little Indian place down the block and splurged on the vindaloo and tandoori vegies with extra Nan to go and went home.

She needed the comfort food and refused to think about her dwindling bank balance or the fact that she just ate. She knew the gallery would be advancing her commission soon, thanks to Gayle, but she hated to let her balance go so low. She knew she had enough canvas and paint to do the other pieces with a margin for error so she could at least push the depressing math aside and focus solely on her nervous stomach.

Megan arrived home and struggled up the stairs with her cumbersome load. She dropped a couple of things on the way and had to backtrack but when she finally reached the kitchen she put the brown bags on the counter with a sigh. She began shoving the perishable stuff in the fridge and started cleaning up the kitchen.

After her cursory once over was finished, Megan pulled out a blue glass bowl from an open shelf of dishes. She put some of the contents of the containers that steamed with curry and spices onto a plate with the Nan and poured a glass of water in case she couldn't take the heat. She took her plate and the box of tandoori into the living room and put the meal on the coffee table. She kicked off her boots with a groan of pleasure. Her purse was hanging from the door, taunting her. She glared at it for a moment then went over and pulled out the large envelope and put it on the table next to her food. She kept a wary eye on it as she ate, daring it to try and make her lose her appetite.

When her stomach was heavy with food and no longer feeling as if it was trying to claw its way out of her, she leaned over and picked up the infamous packet and spilled its contents onto the couch beside her. The letter from the lawyer was there, along with a smaller envelope containing two open-ended roundtrip plane tickets on Air Lingus, a pamphlet for an inn in Galway, a list that included car services, instructions for obtaining a passport and another list of what to pack along with an expense form. Among the contents were also directions to the lawyer's office, and an obituary.

Megan picked the last up with deference and fear. Hear stomach began to hurt and she grabbed the last piece of the cold, flat bread and shoved it in her mouth, chewing furiously to push down the acidic anxiety that was bubbling up in her gut.

The picture was of a handsome man with haunted eyes. The clipping read;

Rev. Johnathan Lucas Donovan
January 12th, 1965 – August 28th, 2014

Formerly of Gardner, Massachusetts, U.S.A. and Clifden, Galway, Ireland. Rev. Johnathan Lucas Donavan, Rev. Luke to his friends and congregation. He is survived by his daughter, Megan Black of Massachusetts. Reverend Donovan was loved by all.

His work in the community and for charity were his legacy. He spent his life in service to God. Reverend Donavan lost his battle to pancreatic cancer but will not be remembered for his illness but for his service to God and the people of he touched with his kindness.

Even though ill, Rev. Luke used his time in the cancer ward to comfort other patients, set up a support group for families, and raise funds for more toys in the children's wing. In lieu of flowers, you are asked to please send donations to St. Brigit's Parish in Galway or donate your time at St. Jeans Hospital or anywhere else.

Reverend Luke? Megan couldn't believe what she was reading. Her father, the asshole that slept with her mother and knocked her up and disappeared without a trace was some sort of holy man? The article looked like it was written about a saint.

Was the sonofabitch in Galway the whole time and just ducking my mother? she wondered. It all had to be a sick joke.

Megan crammed everything but the obituary back in the envelope and brought it to the kitchen with her with a mind to call her mother and ask her why she failed to mention those pieces. She idly wondered if Josie knew more than she said or if it was all lies. She was aware that she was too upset to deal with her at the moment.

"One thing at a time," she told herself, "Just breathe,

Megan. Just breathe. Nothing has changed. You're still the same. Either way you never had a father. What does it matter who he was anyway?"

The feeling of being sucked into a vortex of anxiety and anger subsided as she talked to herself and Megan's heart resumed its natural rhythm. She stuck the clipping to the refrigerator door with a large magnet, so only the picture could be seen, and put the envelope on the counter by the phone to deal with later.

She had already made up her mind that this time she'd call Uncle Ham for the truth since her mother was so reticent to give it to her. She took out the bag of Oreos and began absently eating them as she gazed at the fridge with the picture of a complete stranger who also made up half of her genetics.

He watched her closely. He had promised himself he'd stay away and not stalk her anymore but after two days of hearing the same album blasting on repeat nonstop and the window never closing, Gabriel had become concerned and went to check things out.

What he had seen made his concern even more founded than he had believed. She was working furiously on a canvas the same size as the last he saw although he couldn't see what she was painting as her easel faced the window. He could see that as she painted she would intermittently burst into tears and double over as if in pain before seeming to overcome her sadness and resume her brush strokes.

She painted barefoot in her nightgown. He had the notion that her sadness only added to the ethereal quality of her beauty. Her long hair was knotted at the back of her head and a paintbrush was stuck through the middle of the bun to hold it in place. She had dark circles under her eyes and he could see the tracks on her cheeks where her tears had streamed. He reluctantly looked away from her and gazed around the apartment. The coffee table was littered with empty plates and chip bags and cookie packages and take out boxes. He wondered if she had made her way through all her food yet. From the way she had been working, he doubted she'd bother going out to the store or even bother to call for delivery until the spell that bound her to the canvas was broken.

He had wondered once again why she had been crying. That wasn't a normal part of her process. He speculated if it was the subject on the canvas that was making her lachrymose. Or maybe she was jilted by a lover. That thought darkened his mood and made his fists bunch. He had never seen another man in her apartment besides that boy who fetched the paintings and he had serious doubts that Megan's interest would go in that direction but he still felt the sting of possessiveness and jealousy take hold of him for a moment.

He wished that he could just go to her and wrap his arms around her. He would cradle her head against his chest as her tears spilled across his heart. He would kiss her until she forgot her pain as she became lost in only him.

Shit. I need to stop thinking like this! he told himself and shook his head at his own wayward thoughts. He kept his vigil over her until the sun began to turn to embers.

Megan had passed out on the sofa long after the witching hour and he had covered her with the chenille spread that she kept draped over the back. He smoothed the hair off her porcelain forehead before planting a kiss there. She didn't stir. She looked peaceful and young as she slept and he felt a protective tightness in his chest that stole his breath away.

Boldly, Gabe crept silently to the kitchen area and opened Megan's fridge. It was empty. He closed it quietly and noticed the newspaper clipping hanging there. He removed the magnet and read the obituary, wondering who Reverend Donovan was to her and if the piece of paper was somehow the reason for her tears. He placed the obituary back carefully the same way he found it and leapt out of the open window as quiet as a shadow.

CHAPTER 6

Over the next week, Megan had managed to finish four more pieces. It was a new record for her and she felt giddy if not a little exhausted.

One painting was of the park scene she had sketched and another of the bridge at night, one a sunrise over the fairways and the last was of the sun going down over the same scene in *Nightwatch*. They all four were magnificent works individually. Megan felt magnificent as well although if anyone looked in on her, they'd know that Megan had barely slept in the last few days and had only eaten little more than what she had picked up on the way back from the pub the week before.

She assumed that she must have a guardian angel watching over her because someone had sent a huge basket of muffins one morning and pizza a couple of nights later. Both times, the person making the delivery said it was paid for anonymously. Megan guessed that Gayle had sent them and silently sent up a prayer of thanks her friend.

"I've got to get out of here," Megan said to no one as she angled the light over the canvases that lined her walls.

She could smell herself and the smell wasn't pretty. She hadn't changed from her nightgown or showered at all in at least a week, nor had she brushed her teeth. They felt fuzzy. She felt like what she assumed her mother did after a bender. Stinky and tired and hurting.

Megan put on a pot of coffee and ate the last muffin in the basket before getting in the shower. It was a little hard on the outside, gone stale from sitting out but she ate it with due gratitude.

Once she finished shaving off the week's growth from her legs, bikini line and underarms she felt much better. She stayed under the spray until the hot water started to become warm and got out to towel off. She lotioned her legs and arms and picked her way through her clothes, deciding by the smell of some to do some laundry.

Megan was lucky enough to have her own appliances on suite and stuffed the washer with as much of the offending garments as she could fit. After clicking on the machine, she made her way back to her closet to continue her search for something to wear that was appropriate and clean for her celebratory night out.

Someone put a bottle of water in front of Megan. She looked up to see that striking face of her dreams again. She thought maybe she wouldn't see him again for the rest of her life but apparently he, or fate, had other plans. He sat next to her on the sofa. His entire side was pressed to hers because of his large frame. She tried to scoot over without being offensive. She leaned to the coffee table in front of them and reached for her purse. It was a perfect excuse to move away just enough to regain her equilibrium from the jolt that coursed through her when they touched.

Megan typically didn't like anyone touching her and although she danced really close with him that one night, the only thing that had kept her mind from the close contact of his body had been the music. At least that's what she tried to tell herself. She found herself heating with a blush as she recalled the oh-so-real fantasy she had had of him when she was alone that night at her place.

She pulled a box of slim black clove cigarettes from the bag in her lap and a silver lighter and lit one up. She normally didn't smoke but she liked the smell and esthetics of them and needed something to do with her hands to keep stop her from fluttering nervously.

Feeling more comfortable now that she had a distraction, she looked up into that beautiful face, feeling more composed. The first thing she noted was that his cheekbones looked as though they were carved from the smoothest ivory.

His dark brows arched gracefully over catlike eyes of slate the likes of which she'd ever seen. She recalled that the irises had more grey the previous time she'd seen him though at that moment they looked like a winter storm on the Atlantic. He had full pink lips with a perfect cupid's bow that looked like they were always ready to smile although she had no way of knowing that they rarely did so. He had a dimple in his left cheek and a slightly cleft chin. His hair was a dark brown, with gold threads throughout and where the light caught it she noted that it also had traces of red in it like aged mahogany. It hung back this time in a thick ponytail that ended between his massive shoulder blades. She looked down his corded neck to his broad chest. His shirt parted enough in the front that she could see his sculpted pecs and the light dusting of hair.

He chuckled softly and Megan whipped her head up so fast that her neck hurt.

"Huh?" she asked.

"Are you even listening or am I just eye candy?" he asked her.

"Sorry," Megan murmured, turning scarlet when she saw the humor on his face.

He must have been talking to her for quite a while and all that time she was examining him like he was a sculpture in a freaking museum, oblivious to what he was saying.

He completely ignored her embarrassment and simply smiled at her, not remarking on her tomato colored skin and asked again, "I said, do you always go around pretending strangers are your boyfriends?"

"Not often," she answered tartly.

She was avoiding looking at him at all in case she got lost in him again and was instead trying to concentrate on the smoke curling around her fingers.

"Well then" he continued, "do you often just leave your boyfriends after you're done with them?"

Megan didn't even know what to say. He was either being extremely rude or she was. It had occurred to her she hadn't even asked him his name. *Was it too late for introductions?* she wondered.

"No?" he guessed for her.

Megan's burgundy lips gaped. She was having trouble focusing on what he was saying while having her own inner dialogue. She had never been so confounded by anyone in her life and was worried that it had less to do with how sleep deprived she was and more to do with the strange connection she felt to him. That part scared her. She didn't know him. There was no reason for her to feel this electric current flowing between them. No reason to feel as if he were hers. These feeling weren't rational. They were dangerous. He was dangerous.

"Well, do you often dance with a man and disappear into the night without so much as your name?"

Gabe already knew her name but he found himself ache for the familiarity to come from her lips. For her to open to him in real life and not just when she wasn't aware he was watching. She seemed like she wasn't interested in a conversation with him at all.

"Listen," she began and held up a hand.

She had only picked up bits and pieces of what he'd said. She avoided looking him in the eyes and instead looked at her own hands as she spoke. Her nails were unpolished and her habit of biting them was apparent.

"Gabe," he provided with a grin as if he had read the question in her mind.

"Listen, Gabe. I appreciate you helping with that creep that night and I appreciate the water," she hadn't touched the bottle in front of her, "And I am sorry I was rude but I'm here with my friends," she said pointing over to the couple draped over each other at the bar.

"So, are you telling me you're a lesbian then?" he asked not so innocently.

She wanted to hit him. She wasn't a violent person and didn't even condone violence of any sort but suddenly she wanted to haul off and smack his perfect face. Not only was he ignoring her brush off but this arrogant man was teasing her. Her face grew hot again although this time with anger. Megan was dumbfounded. She couldn't even come out with something scathing to say in retort. He seemed to think her sputtering was humorous and continued to smile that half-cocked smile at her as if he didn't notice her discomfort, however clear it was.

"If I was would you leave me alone?" she asked after a minute.

"If you were what?" he asked her as if he had no idea of what she was speaking.

"If I was gay?" she asked him seriously.

He appeared as if he were giving it some thought. He put a long finger to the crease in his chin. After a moment he answered.

"Well, what kind of person would that make me? If I'm anything I'm open minded. Besides," he added, "I can tell you're not by the way you reacted in my arms and you checking me out and by your nervousness now. I can feel you shaking by the way," he looked her straight in the eyes as he said this and she squirmed a little further away in her seat.

Listening to him talk was like music, even when he was teasing. Megan wondered where that thought came from. She was beginning to think her brain had been turned to pudding and that she should've just stayed home and gone to bed. She could see that he was still awaiting her answer.

"What if I told you I am just a very private person?" she asked.

"Then I would tell you that I respect your privacy but that I wished you would let me know at least one personal thing about you," he responded, "You being my girlfriend and all."

"What's the one thing?" Megan was intrigued.

"Anything you wish, I suppose would do as long as it's something you've never told anyone before. I find myself enchanted by you Megan and will take anything I can get."

He flashed her a pearly grin.

She loved the way he said her name and wondered if she was being so obstinate as a way to avoid considering her attraction to him as something to pursue. There was no room in her life for a man. At least that's what she told herself and others if they asked why she was single.

"You can think about what while we dance," he told her as he took her hand and led her onto the floor.

It was the same song they had danced to the first night. Angel. Megan felt like she was the one enchanted. Being close to him in the dimness, with the romantic music playing and his hands on her hips as they swayed together felt like heaven on earth. She felt drunk although she hadn't any alcohol, only Coke with grenadine and cherries. She sighed into his chest and let her fingers toy with the curls of his ponytail.

Gabriel could feel himself stiffen against her stomach as she gyrated against him to the song. He couldn't pull away from her even if he wanted to, and God help him, he didn't. He was afraid to speak for fear of bringing her defenses back up, so he simply put his cheek to her raven locks and enjoyed the feel of her velvet-clad body pressed closed to him. She smelled sweet like vanilla and clove.

"Have dinner with me tonight," he requested as the song ended. He knew he couldn't just allow her to pull away and disappear again, "You can eat while you think of the one thing you're going to tell me."

"It's a little late for dinner," she hesitated.

"I know a place. It has an amazing view. Maybe you can…" Gabe had almost slipped and said she could paint it.

She had paid it not heed when he had accidentally used her name without her telling him but he needed to be more careful not to reveal how much he knew about her. He wasn't even sure why he was about to invite her to his home in the first place when they could surely find an open restaurant. It was only ten thirty after all.

"Maybe another time," she offered and he knew he had let her slip through his fingers once more.

Gabe bent down and grazed her cheek with his lips as he whispered in her ear, "I'll give you a week. Meet me here next Friday," and backed off into the crowd until she could no longer see him.

Megan wanted to get straight to work when she returned to her apartment that evening. Unfortunately, that plan was thwarted when she found herself daydreaming about Gabe again.

She had placed a large blank canvas on her easel and opened the window. She stripped off the plum velvet dress and put on a large, paint splattered t-shirt and began prepping the canvas. Her thoughts kept darting back to him as she squeezed paint onto pallets and fetched brushes and rags.

By the time she was finished with her preparations, she still couldn't get Gabe off her mind. She went over to the window to find her inspiration, but instead of any bright ideas for her next piece she saw only him. She found that she couldn't see the panorama before her for it was blocked by recollections of eyes of quicksilver that changed to blue when smiling and of sensuous lips that looked like pink satin. After more failed attempts at finding her muse, Megan gave in and let him fill her mind.

She got up and put some music on her iPod and began swaying by herself. She recalled the feel of his large palms resting on her hips and the feeling of her body melded to his as he held her to him as if by some magnetic force. She evoked his spicy scent of bergamot and leather and something uniquely him. As she danced with her eyes closed it became easier to bring him to life there with her in her mind as she did when creating her art. When it felt as though he were there with her, she switched from memory to pure imagination.

Gabe was inching up her t-shirt and kneading her hips with his graceful fingers as they danced. He pulled it up over her head and pressed her body to his as they ground together to the music. He whispered a lyric from the song in her ear, ruffling stray strands of hair and tickling her neck.

"Let me love you," he murmured as he reached up and pulled the paintbrush from her bun, her raven tresses spilling down her bare shoulders. He wrapped his hands in the silky mass and bent down and sighed against her lips and repeated his request, "Let me love you, Megan," and covered her mouth with his.

Their kiss deepened and became more eager. They were pawing each other wildly. Megan was tearing at his clothes trying to remove the barriers keeping them apart. When the last of his garments were shed, Gabe reached down and cupped her voluptuous derriere and lifted her to him. She wrapped her legs around his waist as his slid her down his length in one deft movement. She cried out breathlessly.

"Did I hurt you?" he hesitated, concerned.

"Not at all," she moaned and began moving against him.

Soon the room was filled with groans and sighs as Gabe pressed Megan's back to the wall and began pumping into her in earnest. She had locked her ankles together and was holding onto his neck for dear life as he drove her higher and higher toward the peak of ecstasy.

"You are so beautiful," Gabe said as she climaxed savagely against him.

When the tremors ceased, he carried her over to the bed and laid her upon it. He did nothing more than stare at her for what seemed like an eternity, before she reached up and put her hand on the back of his head, pulling him down for another kiss. They made love until the sun came up.

These dreams were becoming too vivid, Gabe thought when he woke the next morning to find himself nude and feeling oddly replete. It appeared that once again Megan had stolen into his slumber and captured his lustful imagination. If only he could hold her like that in real life just once, he could live an eternity as a happy man.

Megan arose sometime around noon in quite a chipper mood. She was humming to herself all the way to the bakery. On the way back she was so lost in her high spirits that she almost walked into a telephone pole and found herself saying, "excuse me," to it before realizing it wasn't a person. That made her giggle at herself but she kept humming all the way to her door.

The coffee tasted divine with the fresh croissants and strawberry jam she had purchased. She allowed herself to savor them by the window and let her joy be her muse. The trees were dressing up for the autumn in shades of vermillion, amber and gold with frills of jade and the September was beaming its pale yellow in a sky of brilliant azure. It was perfect.

Megan popped the last bit of croissant in her mouth, took a final swig of her coffee, and got to work. She worked long into the night, the image frozen in her mind like a photograph in front of her.

"Gayle, I think you should come over," Megan said

to the answering machine on the other side of the line sometime after nine the next morning.

She had the five complete pieces lined up against the wall in order, leaving the easel empty for the first time in what seemed like months.

An empty easel meant that Megan had spent the day cleaning her apartment vigorously from top to bottom. She mopped the hardwood floors and waxed them, cleaned the windows, dusted, and did all the laundry. She had bleached and scrubbed every surface of her bathroom. She had even scrubbed the grout between the tiles with a toothbrush.

She had gone to the grocers and did a whole shopping and stopped at the liquor store for a couple of bottles of wine for meals she planned on cooking.

She came home to fill her cabinets and restock the freshly cleaned refrigerator. She put the bouquet she purchased into a vase and brewed a fresh pot of French vanilla. While she waited for the pot to fill, she set out some Vienna fingers on a Blue Willow plate that she had bought at a flea market with her mother the previous summer.

Gayle rang the buzzer just as Megan was setting out the mugs. She got up and went down to answer the door.

"Hey, Megs! You're positively glowing! What's the haps?" her friend buzzed.

Megan reached out and hugged the tall woman and ushered her inside.

"At least wait 'til you get up to the apartment before we get into it for Christ's sakes Gayle," although she was laughing as she said this.

Gayle took her seat on the couch and picked up the mug of black coffee and a cookie. She had just taken a bite when she noticed the canvases lining the west wall and spit the Vienna finger onto the floor.

"Holy shit Megan!" she exalted as she rose to go over to the pieces.

"You like them?" Megan beamed.

She could tell Gayle liked them from the way she was looking at them and rubbing her hands together in the way she always did when she was about to make money.

"They seriously are fucking fabulous Megan," she deadpanned, "We need a date for the showing," she added, this last more to herself than Megan.

"That's the other thing I wanted to talk to you about Gayle," she cut in.

"Oh no, you don't, Megan Black! You are NOT

getting out of this showing! No fucking way! I know I've let you put it off…"

Megan cut her short so that she didn't waste her breath on the rant she was working herself up to.

"Gayle, I'm doing the showing. It's not that. Can you sit down, please? You're making me nervous."

Gayle sat down in the wingchair and combed her fingers through her hair, causing it to stick up like pink-tipped porcupine quills. Megan returned to the couch. She stuffed a cookie in her mouth before handing Gayle the manila envelope that contained her dilemma.

Gayle reached down to her chest and put on the reading glasses that hung from a chain there. After a moment she looked up at her best friend.

"Oh, Megs," she sighed and scrutinized the papers once more, "When are you supposed to leave?"

"Not sure. By mid-October, I think but wait. That's not all."

Megan got up and went to the fridge and removed the magnet from the clipping. She handed it to Gayle on her way back to the sofa. She helped herself to another cookie as she watched the shock register on her friend's face before she carefully buried it and looked up blankly. Gayle was waiting for Megan to say what she thought on the subject first.

She obliged.

"I know. It's completely screwed up Gayle. It's fucked, really. I thought that my dad was dead all this time but I get to find out that he wasn't only long enough to find out that he didn't give a shit while he was. And he called himself a man of God. Not very Jesus like if you ask me. Now he's dead and wants to give me something. I doubt it's eighteen years' worth of child support and birthday gifts. I'm not sure what could make up for what he did to my Ma and me but I sure as shit hope I don't have to travel all that way just to get a freaking copy of a bible," Megan was both sobbing and laughing when she finished.

Gayle came over and sat beside her on the couch. She patted her hands on Megan's back in a circular motion.

"Are we laughing or crying Megs?" she asked seriously.

"Both," Megan said through a hiccup.

"Okay. So your mom shagged a priest huh? Why am I not surprised?"

Megan made a snuffling noise.

"I wonder they met while he was performing an

exorcism on her," Gayle jibed and just like that the tide turned. Both girls erupted into a fit of raucous laughter.

"That would be classic Josie Black," Megan roared, clutching her sides.

"Meg, do you think he kept that collar thing on when they did it?" Gayle asked seriously and they exploded again.

"Tell the truth and shame the de'il Meg or I'll drag ya ta confession me-self!" she perfectly imitated her mother's brogue and it sent tears of mirth streaming down both women's faces.

"I wonder if the that's where I was conceived," Megan could barely get this out because she was laughing so hard, "In a confessional."

"Did you hear that one about the priest who walked into a bar?" Gayle began and Megan had slid from the sofa to the floor and rolled around, giggling and snorting uncontrollably. The whole thing was just too ridiculous.

"Stop it, Gayle, I'm going to wet my pants," Megan begged.

"Fine. Fine. My sides hurt anyway. I wonder if that makes your mother the antichrist though. That sure would explain a lot."

Megan almost didn't make it to the bathroom after

Gayle said that last part.

When she returned to the living room she was breathing normally. She drank some coffee and curled up her legs on the sofa.

"So you see why I'm concerned about the showing, right Gayle?" she said reasonably.

"Yes, I can see that," the woman answered, "Let me see what I can do. I can probably get the PR out there and set it up for next weekend. I know that it's already Monday but we can get the pieces in the showroom today. I'll make some calls and get some buyers together and currier the invites for the guest list. We'll also go underground to drum up some interest and up your cred. Don't worry about it. You'll need to look your best and be on your best behavior. I'll need you at the gallery all three nights of the actual gala which would be Thursday, Friday, and Saturday at seven pm sharp. You'll need to put on your social face for all three. Be aloof if you like but not rude. Your pieces will be sharing space with another artist that I have just picked up. Nothing like your stuff at all. Totally different. Sculptor. It will serve as a nice contrast and make your pieces stand out but the showing is all yours Meg. You'll be the highlight. I'll have Billy and Warren come and pick up these five this afternoon."

"Thanks, Gayle," Megan hugged her.

"No problem kiddo," she clapped her hands together signaling that business was done and turned to Megan once more.

"Now, let's talk about me," she said and the women sat back and caught up on what was going on in the world of Gayle.

CHAPTER 7

Megan was so nervous that she thought she would vomit. The first night of the showing was quiet and low key. It was mostly family and friends, art students and people off the street who had nothing better to do as they waited for their dinner reservations. Her Ma and Uncle Ham had even come out to check out her work. They were super proud and it showed.

Uncle Ham had even proclaimed that every piece was, "Bloody Brilliant!"

He had even offered to buy one until Megan whispered in his ear the price.

"Oh, that wounds me, Meg," he said as he clutched his chest dramatically, "I can afford it for sure lass, but the Irish in me won't allow such a cost even for such a masterpiece as this. Couldn't you give a discount to your old Uncle?"

Megan couldn't help but laugh and promise, "I'll paint you a special piece Uncle Ham and you can put it in the bar with all the other special pieces I've done for you."

Uncle Ham had begun displaying Megan's artwork since preschool and had since graduated from hanging the crayon colored construction paper stick figures to letting her paint the mural that covered an entire wall of the bar back when she was in high school.

"Thank ya, Meg!" he beamed, "But it's a pub, not a bar. You should know the difference," he reminded her for the hundredth or so time.

Megan had spent the better part of the previous Wednesday with Josie, going from store to store on Mass Ave. trying to pick out at least one dress for `the event. Somehow, her Ma had convinced her that she needed a new coat and shoes as well as some lingerie. So much for going braless, Megan thought.

The coat was easy. They found a long, thick woolen coat of burgundy with buttons carved of silver and laced up the back. The lining was black satin and Megan was in love. She almost died when she saw the price tag.

"Six hundred bucks is a lot of cash for a coat, Ma!" she whispered furiously in her ear.

She wasn't embarrassed that someone would hear

how cheap she was. Six hundred would cover most of her rent. She did regret it though as she was cautious of making Josephine cause a scene. To Megan's surprise, she didn't.

"You need a good coat, Meg. I know you want ta act as if I picked it out for ya but 'twas all you girl. Besides, you'll be needin' a good coat. It gets just as cold in Éire as it does here. Damp too," she informed her quietly.

Josephine was being totally reasonable and Megan felt like a total brat.

"You'll be wantin' it but you want it for less then, yes?" it wasn't a question.

"I don't think this boutique is the type of place that haggles Ma." She rolled her eyes at the older redhead.

"Weel now, we'll see about that, won't we?" Josephine went over to the counter with the coat and began talking with the sales woman. They were both bent with heads bowed over the garment, examining it. The blonde saleswoman stepped back and called another woman named Susan from the back room and they all went back to talking. Megan watched Josie hand over her credit card to the woman and it was swiped. The coat was draped with a garment bag and they were off.

"Sixty percent off," Josie told her daughter proudly

before she could ask.

"More than half price? How'd you manage that?" Megan asked, shocked.

Josephine smiled radiantly, "I showed them how there were a few stitches off and that one of the buttons was loose ta boot. I told them I just wanted ta point it out and ask if they had another in that size, mind I knew they wouldn't, places like this only stock one or two of the same style, and when they told me no I offered ta take it off their hands but only at a discount since my daughter would likely ta only be able to wear it no but the once before the whole ting fell apart. I also mentioned that you needed it for yer big gala tonight. Even added how I hoped none of yer hoity-toity society friends saw the ting unravelin' and promised that you'd tell them ya had it fer a while yet but also where you got it from. I also promised that if the sale went badly you'd mention that too."

"Thanks, Ma!" Megan said as she clasped the older woman's shoulders and pulled her in for a hug.

"Now we go ta Saks for the dress," her mother directed, triumphantly.

The previous night with her mom and Ham had only

been a warm up. A test run. Megan knew that this night was the real deal. She patted her belly through the black satin of the gown she wore and wished that the caterers would hurry up and fill the silver trays with puff pastries before she developed an ulcer. Megan loved the feel of the cool satin of her dress on her skin, although she would have been able to enjoy it better if she wasn't forced by both Gayle and Josephine to wear proper undergarments. She had, like a good girl, donned the black satin corselet, complete with garters and stockings and even a small lace thong. Megan didn't get the point of wearing underwear that didn't look like underwear but after looking in the mirror, she was forced to admit that the esthetics were very pleasing. She felt like a black haired bombshell.

After donning the dress she felt even sexier. It had a portrait neckline and it hugged her curves like an hourglass before plunging out to the floor. It had a slit on the side, hidden beneath the folds that would only be visible when she was walking. The low, silver Valentino sling-backs that had maxed out her credit and a pair of small sterling hoops completed the ensemble.

"You look like sex on heels," Gayle told her as she

approached with a champagne flute in one hand and a napkin with hors d'oeuvres in another.

"Please tell me that those are for me!" Megan begged.

"Of course."

She handed the nervous woman the napkin and the flute obligingly.

"You should eat while you can. It's going to be a long night and it'll be hard to flag down someone with a tray while you're flanked by critics and connoisseurs," she warned.

Not even a heartbeat later, Megan Black was surrounded. She answered questions from every direction.

Until an older woman with an iron perm and a dress with shoulder pads had pointed them out, Megan hadn't even realized that the gallery, or more aptly Gayle, had brought in some of her older pieces, most of which had already been gifted or purchased and some that had just never sold. One wall was filled with her older art and the others held the newer pieces. On a central curtain-wall stood *Nightwatch*. There were sculptures on pedestals here and there that Megan assumed were from that new artist that Gayle had mentioned. There was a lot of oohing and ahhing over the canvases and Megan found it hard to stay focused on the conversations the society types were trying to have with her. Gayle had come to her rescue numerous times as she fretted like a mother duck over her hatchlings.

The food dwindled and so did the throng and Megan's feet were aching from the heels.

Gayle and Diane came over to congratulate her on her successful showing.

"That was quite the turnout," Diane said, impressed.

"Every piece was sold," added Gayle as she rubbed her palms together, "I'd say you made roughly eighty-five k tonight, after the gallery's cut. Not bad for your first showing."

"Holy fucking shit!" Megan squeaked.

"No kidding," said Gayle.

"Who bought the pieces?" Megan asked.

She wanted to make sure her babies were going to good homes regardless of what seemed to be an outrageous amount of money that was coming to her.

"Some of the older stuff that wasn't spoken for went to a couple of hags who are regular customers of the gallery. Staunch art supporters. You met them.

The main pieces, *Nightwatch, Daydream, Sleeping City, Boston Rising, Night's Edge* and *Daybreak* all went to one buyer."

Megan arched a raven brow when Gayle told her this.

"One buyer? I have a fan?" she demanded of her friend.

"I'd say so, and a wealthy one too. You'll get to meet him in a moment."

Gayle turned behind her and waved her hand to a man standing in the corner.

Megan almost swooned with surprise when Gabe walked over to join their little group, his dimple belying the smile that he was stifling.

"Gabriel, it's my pleasure to introduce you to our artist, Megan Black," Gayle said formally.

She obviously didn't recognize him from the club, Megan thought. Maybe it was the custom-tailored Armani suit that had thrown her off or the sleek ponytail he had pulled his hair back into, revealing cheekbones like cut glass and cleanly shaven skin marked only by sculpted sideburns.

Instead of admitting to their acquaintance, Gabe clasped her hand and brought it to his sensuous lips and placed a kiss on her palm, "It's a pleasure, Miss Black."

Megan was rooted to the spot. She could still feel where his lips branded her after he withdrew and felt a warm pool between her legs in answer. She knew she should say something but couldn't find the words. Luckily for her, Gayle saved her.

"The gallery is extremely grateful for your patronage as I'm sure Miss Black is as well," Gayle elbowed her in the ribs covertly.

"Yes. Thank you," Megan stammered without meeting his gaze.

He still hadn't dropped her hand. He held it casually in his. It felt warm and dry in her cold one and was making her knees weak although it was oddly comforting. This was a rightness to it that she couldn't explain.

Diane and Gayle were shooting each other furtive glances beside them, trying to telepathically convey that something was going on there and that neither knew what it was. They both just continued silently watching the exchange between the man and their friend, waiting for some sort of clue.

"You're welcome Megan," he said her name familiarly, "I'd have been grateful to have just one

Megan Black in my bedroom."

She coughed and spluttered, "Sorry. Champagne bubbles," as if that explained her reaction.

She was caught off guard for a moment. Surely he knew how he sounded. He put so much heat behind the one comment it was if he had purchased nude self-portraits of her. Or just her. Nude.

"Now I can lie in bed and stare at all of her pieces for as long as I want whenever I please," he added innocently.

Much to her chagrin, Megan found herself picturing what his bedroom looked like and what it would be like to have him lying in bed staring at her body with his lazy blue eyes though she was fairly certain that was the reason for him commenting with such innuendo in the first place. Did he have to be such a charming jerk? She wondered.

"They'll be delivered on Monday evening, as we've agreed. You've made a fine investment Mr..." Gayle was fishing for his last name.

"Just call me Gabriel or Gabe. No need for formality Gayle," he avoided her probing smoothly.

"Just make sure you tell the boys where you want them placed Gabe," she said and shook his hand, forcing him to release his grip on Megan's. She felt like she lost her anchor.

"Well, I have some other guests to attend to. I'm sure they'll be disappointed that you poached the best pieces from right under their noses. I'm sure a few feathers were ruffled. It was a pleasure doing business with you Gabe," she shook his hand once more before linking her arm in Diane's and heading off in the direction of another group that had gathered by *Nightwatch* with their near empty glasses.

"I thought they'd never leave," Gabe smiled, relieved.

He took her hand once more.

"I can't believe you bought all six pieces," Megan revealed her astonishment. She wasn't sure what game he was playing or even if she'd be able to keep up if she could. She wanted to trust him but her gut was telling her that something wasn't adding up. She asked suspiciously, "How'd you even know about the gala?"

"I've been stalking you," he stated baldly.

Megan's hand jolted and she looked up to search his handsome face. The amusement there was evident.

"You're teasing me," it was a statement.

His dimple deepened and his eyes twinkled blue

with his amusement.

"Maybe a little," he acknowledged, "Now when can you get out of here so we can go have our night out?" he asked, the mask of seriousness slipping over his features and casting him in marble once more.

"I forgot all about that," she admitted as she pinkened to the most becoming shade of rose.

"Well, it's a good thing that I didn't," he said.

They said their farewells soon after. He helped her don her new coat in the most gentlemanly fashion. He tucked her arm into the crook of his and headed for the street.

"I don't suppose you want to walk in those heels," he supposed.

His notice of her discomfort was oddly sweet to Megan.

"Yeah, they are killing me but I supposed there is no beauty without pain," she said, quoting the old adage.

He looked at her curiously for a moment as if he were about to say something. He appeared to have changed his mind and said instead, "Megan, you'd be beautiful even if you were barefoot and in rags."

The ferocity in which stated the complement was a surprise and Megan blushed again. He seemed pleased with that response and she felt the strange urge to please him even more. She put most of her weight on his arm and lifted a foot and removed a shoe. She had almost lost her balance for a moment but he caught her around the waist.

"Here, let m," he said against her hair as he steadied her.

Gabe bent down on one knee and lifted her other foot onto his lap, forcing her to hold on to his broad shoulders for support. He slid a hand up the hem of her dress and traced the line her stockinged calf down to her ankle before pulling off the other shoe. He dropped it to the ground and dug the heel of his palm into her arch. Megan groaned audibly and flashed pearly white teeth up at her. He gently lowered her foot to the pavement and picked up the shoe, rising slowly as he did so. Megan hadn't let go of his shoulders and that made it all the more easy for Gabe to dip his head and brush a kiss across her lips. She closed her eyes instinctively and parted her lips in expectation of his tongue but it never came. Her lashes fluttered open and she met his gaze, emerald to molten silver. She slowly unwound her hands from his neck and took a deep breath and backed away a couple of steps. He handed her the shoe and she took it dumbly.

"Milady," he proffered his arm once more and she took it.

"Thanks," she blushed out.

Gabe's original plan was to take her to his place but he wasn't sure if it was the right time yet. Instead, he decided on letting her choose.

"Where to Cinderella?" he had asked and she had led them to a barbeque joint that she knew would be opened.

She had put her shoes back on while on the steps before entering, using the railing this time and he couldn't help but smile at her cautious nature. She should be cautious. Megan would be a fool not to notice the electricity that sizzled in the air when they touched. The danger of a lightning strike was a very real threat. He was a very real threat.

"I don't know if there is anything sexier than a beautiful woman in an evening gown eating ribs with her bare hands," Gabe remarked sometime later as they dined.

Truth be told, he wasn't sure if it was just her that made everything look so damned good. She was truly a magnificent creature. Her delicate hands moved over everything with grace and purpose. He couldn't help but think of them on his body and when she licked barbeque sauce off her fingers, he'd thought he'd be undone completely.

"Is that because of the phallic shape, do you suppose?" she wondered aloud.

Gabe hadn't even thought of that aspect but now couldn't tear his errant mind away from the thought. He was thoroughly distracted from his own food and instead nursed the beer in his hand.

"Perhaps," he offered, sounding cooler than he felt.

The truth was he thought his pants would catch fire at any moment.

"I'm glad to hear that it's not a total turn-off to see me eating. It seems that on every date I've been on, the guy expects me to order a small salad and some water and eat it in tiny bites like a gerbil. I don't believe in perpetuating the lie that women don't eat plus I *love* food. Always have, so I never really cared to keep up the pretense even though my humanness in that aspect has been pointed out and certainly hasn't gotten me a second date with most of them," she shrugged as if to say, "oh well" and looked over the half-eaten rib at him to gage his response to her statement.

"Well, I guess you date a lot of idiots then," he said

and she smiled, her mouth full of food.

They talked a lot about nothing in general and enjoyed each other's company during the meal. None of the silences seemed awkward at all, rather, she felt extremely comfortable just being with him.

Gabe paid the tab while she was in the ladies room and helped her into her coat once more. He let her pay the tip as a show of her independence although she thought maybe she was a hypocrite since he had paid for everything else and any money she had was because he bought her paintings. She decided not to think on that. She slipped back out of her Valentino's and they were off again into the night.

"I've had a wonderful time tonight. You're a wonderful woman Miss Black," Gabe told her as they walked hand in hand down the empty Cambridge streets.

"I've had a great time too. I wasn't expecting you to be so...." she couldn't find the word.

"Handsome? Charming? Irresistible? Sexy?" he supplied with a chuckle.

She punched his arm.

"Yes, you're all those things and you know it but I think the word I was looking for was perfect," she admitted truthfully.

Gabe was taken aback at her candor. She thought he was perfect? This perfect woman thought he, Gabriel, was perfect. His heart beat oddly in his chest. He turned her to face him. There were no words so he took her beautiful face with both hands and kissed her deeply.

CHAPTER 8

Megan dropped her shoes on the floor as she floated in as if on a cloud. She had had the best night of her life. She wasn't sure if it would've been made better if Gabe had consented to come up for coffee instead of excusing himself like a gentleman with no more than a farewell kiss placed in her palm and one more on her forehead, or if that old world charm and chivalry was perfect enough on its own.

She stripped off the dress and hung it on the hook on the bathroom door. She didn't bother taking off the lingerie. Instead, she went over to the large mirror in her bedroom and admired herself in it. Megan regretted that Gabe didn't get to see what she had been hiding beneath her dress. She had pictured him seeing her like that, hair unbound, pale breasts lifted and heaving above the black satin of her corset. Her tiny waist was accentuated by the boning there and her hips flared out, creating an hourglass. The thong was nothing more than a patch that only covered the landing strip of hair beneath, more of a tease than a concealment. The garters that held the silk stockings in place made her already milky soft thighs seem even more appealing. She ran a hand over the soft mounds of her breasts and imagined Gabe touching her there, just like that. She did the same with her thighs.

She brought Gabe to mind. He was still wearing the Armani suit that she last saw him in and she imagined helping him out of the jacket and slipping her fingers in between the buttons of his crisp white shirt as she kissed his neck. He tasted like spice and smoke and sweet saltiness. She trailed kisses along the shell of his ear and heard him groan when she darted her tongue out to lick the lobe.

Gabe knew this was no dream. He was actually sitting on Megan's bed as she stroked his chest and stuck her hot little tongue in his ear but he had no idea how he got there. One moment he was lying on his bed, fully dressed, thinking of her with a mix of burning and regret and the next he was there with her in her room. He *knew* he had left her at her door. He remembered kissing her goodnight. On the forehead. He knew that because he had berated himself all the way home for not taking one more sip from those sumptuous lips. Regardless of how he got there or if this was a dream or not, Gabe was not stupid enough to get in the way of his own desire for her again that night.

Megan had moved her mouth down the column of his throat and straddled him. He could see himself and her backside in the mirror. She unbuttoned each button on his shirt exquisitely slow, savoring the unwrapping. He shrugged out of it and she ran her fingers through the small patch of hair on his muscled chest and followed the trail of it down his rippling abs. She brought her mouth to his and drank deeply, thrusting her tongue against his in an age old rhythm that echoed in her hips.

He thrust his hands into the silken skein at her back and tugged until she arched back, exposing her throat and breasts for him to feast upon. He released both ivory globes from their constraint by tugging the corset down so that they hung above the top. He bent his head forward and drew one taught bud in his mouth and suckled until she cried out. He drew the other one up in his hand so that he held both close enough that his hot breath could be felt on each sensitive tip, then he went from one to the other and back again, suckling and nipping until she was panting and writhing against him. He could feel her moisture through the front of pants and it egged him on to continue his sweet torture of licking and sucking her nipples until she at last submitted and exploded right there in his lap. He grinned like a big cat who wasn't done toying with his prey. He rolled her beneath him on the bed, pinning her to the mattress with his weight. She ran her fingers feverishly up his back and fisted them in his hair as he kissed her until she was breathless. He kneeled before her to unfasten his pants but she stopped him.

"Let me," she commanded and he obeyed.

He dropped his hands to his waist and she got on her knees before him, displaying her generous backside. She undid his belt and unfastened his fly and let out an audible sound of approval as his manhood sprang forth from his pants. She leaned forward on all fours and rubbed her soft cheek against the satin covered steel of his erection.

He held his breath, stunned by her boldness and the excruciatingly wonderful feel of her petal soft skin on his sensitive member. Megan smiled up at him shyly as she flicked out her tongue and laved at the engorged tip.

Gabe was almost undone.

He fisted his hands in her hair and whispered, "Please," although he wasn't sure if he was begging her to stop or to keep going.

She must have taken it as the latter because she flicked out her tongue again, trailing it all the way from the base to the head before opening her mouth and taking him in.

Gabriel was sweating with the shear restraint he was exercising. He was fighting the instinct to thrust into her sweet, hot mouth as she explored him for the first time with the most intimate of kisses. When she reached up and cupped his balls in her small, smooth hand he almost lost it. He yanked her hair back roughly, pulling her away. Her lower lip quivered slightly and she looked like someone had stolen her lollipop. He pushed her on the bed and spread her legs and cupped her bottom. He looked like a man starved.

"My turn," he said hungrily and bent his head to pay homage to her.

Megan wrapped her fingers in his long hair as a way to anchor herself to this plane while Gabe's playful tongue expertly toyed with the soft pink folds of her womanhood. He lapped lazy circles around her labia before taking the entire bud of her pleasure in his mouth and sucking on it until she screamed and her back came off the bed. He locked one arm around her hips and let the other hand roam up to roll a nipple between two fingers. Megan's pelvis was thrusting to meet the onslaught of his mouth of its own accord. Gabriel pinched the rosy peaks of her breast with one hand, releasing it only long enough to knead the other one. He released his hold on her with the other hand so that he could reach down and slide a finger inside of her. Megan bucked at the intrusion and he began gliding the finger in and out of her soaking entrance, licking in time with the movements. Megan felt a like she was being brought to the brink of all she knew. Her nerve endings were on fire and she felt like she couldn't take much more. When Gabe took her clit into his mouth once more, just as he shoved his finger deep inside of her, she shattered into a million pieces.

Gabe had retracted his hand and was leaning on his elbows watching her face. She was enraptured. He deftly removed his pants all the way and pulled her on top of him. She sat down slowly so that he could feel every inch of himself filling her to her core. She moaned and lolled her head back and he pulled her down for a kiss.

He knew she was waiting for him to take the lead so he took hold of her ass and started sliding her up and down his throbbing cock until she began riding him on her own. Gabe reached up to cup her breasts, tracing circles with his thumbs over the hardened tips as she impaled herself over and over again on him. Gabe knew he wasn't going to last much longer. She was so slick and tight and she fit him like the perfect sheath to his sword.

"Oh, Megan!" he cried out.

"Gabriel!" she answered as they reached the pinnacle together.

Gabriel was at a loss as he woke in his own bed in the morning. He was beginning to think that Megan may be some sort of witch. Her ability to call him to her like that was astounding. He couldn't recall traveling at all. One moment he was in his room, and the next he was in hers.

By her shyness around him, he couldn't imagine that she was aware she was calling him forth or that they were lovers and he found that curious. One thing he noticed so far was that it only happened on the nights they'd actually seen each other. It was a mystery. Gabriel was intent on finding out the answers and he had an inkling where to start. He was going to ask Megan out again and then watch her to see what happened after. See what kind of magic she was using.

That was the most vivid dream that Megan ever had.
She didn't know she possessed such a lewd imagination.
She was certainly a creative person, and she was aware
of what could go on between lovers, but she lacked the
personal experience to ever actually envision so
realistically, acts she had never herself engaged in. She'd
gone to second base with guys before and knew how to
take care of herself but her fantasies had been different
since meeting Gabe. Maybe she was just lonely, she
thought, although that didn't explain the feeling that she
had been ridden hard and put away wet, nor the stains on
the sheets and the cramps in parts she never used. She
stripped out of the lingerie that she had slept in, clicked
on the coffee maker, and went to set a bath.

The knock on the door startled Megan. She wasn't
expecting anyone. She grabbed the baseball bat from the
closet and headed down to the stairs, her bare feet
moving silently on the steps. Through the panes, she
could see that it was Gabe.

"What's he doing here?" she asked herself aloud.
Megan undid the locks and opened the door a crack.

"Can I come in?" Gabe asked.

She couldn't resist the smile he beamed in her direction and she stepped aside to let him in.

Gabe was enjoying the view as he followed Megan up the stairs to her apartment. She was wearing nothing but a long Celtics t-shirt that didn't quite make it to mid-thigh.

"Great place," he said when they walked into the large living room with its eight foot windows.

"I like it," she said over her shoulder.

"I hope I'm not intruding?" he phrased it as a question but she could see that he didn't really care if he was.

"Not at all. Thanks to you buying all my pieces, I didn't have to go to the gallery tonight. Bonus!" her laugh was like tinkling bells and his smile broadened.

"Happy to oblige," he said.

She went over to the small gas stove and began stirring something in a stockpot. He noticed the aroma when he'd come up. It smelled heavenly.

"What's cooking good looking?" he asked as he approached the counter.

She grinned. The phrase seemed silly coming from him.

"Guinness stew. You want some?" she asked.

She had already pulled out two large bowls and some spoons, "There's butter in the fridge for the brown bread. Do you mind grabbing it for me?" she asked as she pulled the loaf from the oven.

"I didn't know you cooked," Gabe confessed as he slathered butter on his third piece of bread sometime later, "It's delicious."

Megan blushed at the compliment, "I don't cook very often. When I do I prefer comfort food," she admitted.

"You're Irish then?" he asked her.

"Actually yes. My mom emigrated here before I was born. I actually grew up in an apartment above a real Irish pub. My Uncle Ham taught me how to make this, although he's not really my uncle."

Mentioning one of her favorite childhood memories made Megan feel warm and fuzzy and she smiled.

Gabe had dropped his piece of bread into his bowl and simply took all that she said in, fascinated. This was the most she'd ever opened up to him and he wondered if it was simply because she was on her own turf that made her so comfortable or was she becoming accustomed to his presence. He wanted to think it was the latter but admitted to himself that it could be the first.

"Have you ever been to Ireland yourself? You have a touch of the accent," she asked him.

"I haven't been back there for a really long time," he answered although he hoped she wouldn't ask exactly how long.

"Did you leave there when you were a kid then? Where were you from?" she asked seriously and he looked at her like she had ten heads.

"Do you still have family there?" she prodded despite his silence.

"I'm an orphan," he answered at last.

It was pretty much the truth and the thought made him feel raw but he hoped she would be able to deduce that as the reason for his reluctance to her probing.

Megan instantly regretted asking that question.

"I'm going to Ireland for the first time soon," she told him. He remained silent so she continued, "I've got some business there but I'm a bit nervous. My mother never liked to talk about home so I only know what I can pull off the internet. I've never even flown before so I'm also a bit nervous about that too although it's pretty exciting to finally get to travel. I've always wanted to."

She was blabbering to feel the awkward silence of his admission and she knew it.

She stuffed some stew in her mouth to shut herself up so that her guest could have a turn to talk only if he chose to. He had already set his empty bowl on the coffee table and when she had gestured for more he had politely held up his palm.

Finally, he asked, "What kind of business do you have in Ireland?"

She chewed it over for a bit before answering, deciding that honesty would probably be best. Her mother always said, *Meg, tis no use ta put on a bonnet on a sheep and call it a lady.*

"My father died. I never met him. I'm a bastard."

She definitely wasn't putting any bonnets on any sheep there. It was a simple fact.

"I'm sorry for your loss," he said kindly, then added, "and his for not getting to spend more time with such an amazing young woman."

What was she supposed to say to that? Megan felt a lonely tear roll down her cheek. Gabe bent across the table and caught it with his thumb. He hated seeing her tears and bent down to kiss them away.

Megan pulled away and rose. Gabe thought he blew it until she crossed the space and sat in his lap. He enfolded her in his arms and put her head on his shoulder and simply held her there, lending her his strength. He felt that primitive urge to keep her safe that she seemed to instill in him with her tears. It was a tightness in his chest that urged him to pull her to him and protect him with his body if necessary.

He stroked her hair as she lay against him, listening to the soothing thud of his heart. She nuzzled his neck and he began to lazily stroke her back. Gabe wondered if she had noticed his erection bulging against his fly beneath her. Every little wriggle caused him to suck in his breath. It was sweet agony to hold her so close with only the thin barriers of fabric separating her sex from his.

Megan felt him straining against his jeans. She tried to keep as still as possible but she felt a restlessness as if his very nearness was prodding her to move. She reached up her hand and began stroking his nape languidly. She felt him stir beneath her and she shifted her hips ever so slightly, searching for some sort of comfort in an area that was becoming intensely uncomfortable.

She looked up shyly from beneath the fan of her lashes. He was staring down at her. His face stony, as if he was concentrating very hard on something. She moved again and he leaned down and crushed her mouth with a kiss. She moaned and rocked on his lap and he reached a hand beneath the t-shirt. He was glad that the path to the juncture of her thighs was unencumbered. He cupped her mons in his hand and she gasped into his mouth. He angled the kiss differently as he began rubbing his fingers back and forth across the most intimate part of her.

"You are so wet," he said against her lips and slipped a finger inside her, rocking his palm against the sensitive nub.

She was panting against him but he held her firm as he circled her clit with her thumb as he pressed his digit firmly against her inner wall, creating an intense pressure that was building in her center. Megan began squirming in earnest. He was playing her body like an instrument. She wanted more. She wanted it all.

"Please," she begged breathlessly against his mouth, "Please. Oh God. I need you, Gabe."

He kept his hand buried between her legs as he unbuttoned his fly with the other. When he was freed from the denim he slid her over him. He let her adjust to his size and pulled the t-shirt over her head. He cupped her breasts from behind and she turned her head so that he could take her mouth. She began undulating her hips as he plunged his tongue intoo her mouth. He reached once more for the place where they were joined and began rubbing. She ground her hips against his, trying to increase the pressure. He put his arm around her belly and deftly flipped their positions so that he was still behind her as she was draped over the arm of the couch. He threw off his shirt and pressed his bare chest to her back and kissed the back of her neck. She met him thrust for thrust. He reached around once more and let her slide back and forth over his fingers as he pistoned into her and she ground her hips back against him.

"Gabriel! Oh God!" she screamed.

He felt her convulse around him and he poured himself into her with a roar.

He lay with her on the couch spoon-style. His cheek against her hair as he stroked the length of her body. He could still feel the small tremors go through her every now and then.

"Mmmh," she sighed. "I'm hungry. Are you hungry?" she asked as she tried to wriggle free.

"Don't get up," he pleaded and lay his muscled arm heavily over her.

"I have to," she said, "Besides, I've gotta pee."

Gabe lifted his arm, releasing her. She scooted off the sofa and padded over to the bathroom. On her way back she took something out of the oven.

"What's that?" Gabe asked as he poked his head up.

"Apple crisp," she said proudly.

She pulled a pint of vanilla ice-cream from the freezer and stuck to spoons inside and headed back to the sofa.

Gabe sat up so that she could scooch in beside him. He pulled her hair back and planted a kiss on the side of her neck.

"I don't need desert when I have something sweet right here," he growled and bit her neck playfully.

Megan was alone in her bed when she woke. She didn't remember passing out. She looked through the apartment but there was no Gabe. The clock in the kitchen read two a.m. She was relieved to see the two spoons in the half-empty pan that held the apple crisp and the two bowls in the sink. She was beginning to think it was all just another dream brought on by her vivid imagination on a lonely night.

Reality struck like a punch to the gut as Megan began washing the dishes. If Gabe really was there and they really did have sex, then he had gotten what he'd wanted and had no reason to stay. She was just another acquisition for him, like her paintings. It must have been a real novelty for him to not only get the art but the artist too, she thought. A real bargain. She pondered if that was how her mother had felt after her father left but reminded herself that even he had stayed for the entire summer.

"Wham bam thank you, mam," Megan said aloud to herself in the mirror as she dried her hands.

Megan set the shower to hot and stepped inside. She was miserable. She felt like a fool. Her first time giving herself to a man and he ducked out the second she had closed her eyes as if he couldn't wait for the chance to escape. The steaming water beaded down on her head as she scrubbed her already pink skin until it hurt. She felt dirty and used. The tears fell, washing over her with the water.

The hot water turned cold and Megan stepped out of the shower, shivering as much from the cold as the shock to her system. She had never felt so lonely in her life, and if anyone knew loneliness it was the child of a drunk single mother. Wanting to simply collapse from misery, she pulled on her nightgown, climbed into bed and curled into a ball and cried herself to sleep.

"God, what am I doing?" Gabe rubbed a hand over his face.

He wasn't sure what he expected to happen, but making love to a bereaved Megan wasn't one of them. Sneaking out in the middle of the night and leaving her alone was another thing that wasn't on that list. He felt like a real asshole, especially since he had had such a good time with her. Not just the sex part but the entire night. He couldn't recall ever going so long without needing to feed. He also couldn't remember the last time he had actually been able to taste food or feel a touch. He had spent centuries unable to receive any sort of pleasure beyond the feed and in the last two weeks, it was if the curse were completely removed.

Gabe still wasn't certain what was happening to him but he was sure that it was somehow connected to her. Megan was the key and thanks to him panicking, would probably never speak to him again.

The amber liquid swirled in the glass as Gabe sat staring at it, pondering everything. He let a sip burn a trail down his throat. He couldn't recall how many nights he had sat alone sampling from the same bottle, knowing it would give no surcease to his gloom. Now he truly had a reason to take up the bottle. The irony of him trying to numb his aching heart was not lost on him. He took another sip. It was amazing nonetheless. Not only could he taste the whiskey, but he could feel the effects and they didn't help to dispel the misery he was feeling. The hazy feeling only seemed to exacerbate his despondency. He fucked up and he knew it. He screwed up royally. He was a coward who ran away. He just couldn't figure out a way to make it right.

He emptied the remnants of the tumbler in one gulp and reached out to set it on the table but the table wasn't there anymore. In its place was a nightstand piled with sketchbook and pencils. The hair rose on the back of Gabriel's neck as it dawned on him where he was. He was in Megan's bedroom again.

CHAPTER 9

They slept nestled together in a cocoon of blankets. She cried out a couple of times for her mother and Gabe patted her hair until she settled and stilled in his arms. The tear-tracks were still fresh on her cheeks when he had arrived.

She had mumbled, "Mm, Gabe, I thought you were gone," before cuddling up against him and snoring lightly.

Pain had fisted itself in his chest. He knew he was the reason for those tears. That she had probably rose and found him gone and had thought the worst. She looked so small and sad and helpless and a fierce protectiveness washed over him. Gabe knew that no matter what she was, that causing her any more pain was not an option. To hurt her would destroy him.

"Is that whiskey?" she asked, her nose wrinkled prettily.

Gabe opened one grey eye and directed it at the woman asking.

"What?" he asked.

She held the glass to her nose and gagged.

"Glenfiddich, yuck!" she held the glass away and made a face.

"You don't like whiskey," he assumed.

He sat up amidst the tangle of blankets and took offending beverage from her hand and placed it back on the nightstand.

"It brings back bad memories," she admitted.

He reached up and rubbed her back between her shoulder blades.

"What, did you get sick from it before?" he queried.

"No. I've never had it before, myself. My mother on the other hand..." she trailed off and shrugged.

Gabe caught her meaning and he wondered exactly kind of suffering she had known in her young life. He thought of her calling out for her mother in the night and wondered if the scent of the whiskey had caused her nightmares.

"I'm sorry," he said simply, trying to encompass the entirety of the situation.

She sighed. The back rub felt really good.

"You didn't know," she waved it off, "But I'm curious. Where'd you get it?"

Gabe took a few beats to answer. The single malt had obviously not come from her cabinet so there was no use there and she obviously had no clue that she was the reason he was there at all ...

"I'm sorry Megan," he said and moved his hand up to massage her nape, "I snuck out of here last night and went home for a bit. I had an important business call and didn't want to disturb you."

The lie sounded plausible to Gabe's ears.

She stiffened. It didn't add up.

"What kind of business are you in that you make calls at two in the morning? And how did you get back in after you went home? The door locks behind you downstairs if you don't set it."

Damn she thinks fast! he cursed to himself. He could be just as quick, though.

"The kind of business that takes place overseas which means meetings with people in different time zones and I took your keys because I didn't want to be locked out. I didn't want to wake you up and I didn't want to leave a note like a dirtbag. I was only gone for about a half hour, an hour, tops," he lied smoothly.

"So why even bother coming back? And why bring a drink with you? Is my company really so terrible that you can't be sober to sleep with me?" she didn't realize that she was hurt that he left at all and the whiskey made her angry.

"Have you lost your mind, Megan?" Gabe asked her seriously.

Her lower lip quivered and she blinked back tears before setting her chin and crossing her arms across her bosom.

He pulled her down onto the pillow with him and wrapped her in his big arms and said, "Sleeping with you, Megan is the single most incredible thing that's happened to me. I didn't want to leave your side but I had to. I never thought things would go that way last night and I was unprepared. You surprised me, Megan. I grabbed the drink out of habit. I typically have one to help me sleep. I was so caught in my routine that I forgot and by then I figured I'd just walk the block with it in my hand although I spilled most on the way."

Gabe had explained everything neatly as possible and she bought it all hook, line, and sinker. She relaxed against him once more. Surrendering back again to trust and his embrace.

"I'm sorry," she said simply.

"For what?" he asked her, surprised.

"For being a bitch to you. I'm not a morning person and I'm not used to guys disappearing in the night," she snuggled closer and he felt himself harden against her backside. The feeling wasn't unpleasant.

"You weren't a bitch, Megan and I'm sure that all the guys you take to your bed aren't as dumb as I was to leave," he said, self -deprecatingly.

She turned to face him, "I haven't taken any other guys to bed so I wouldn't know."

She searched his eyes for his response.

Gabe remembered the blood from the first night. He had thought it was a dream at the time and he tried to hide the shock and anger from his beautiful features.

"No one?" he asked, afraid of the answer.

She traced his dimple.

"Just you," she admitted.

The icy fist in his chest reappeared. He had taken her innocence like some sort of beast in the field. To make it worse, he had lied to her. Not only about the previous night but everything. His entire existence was a lie. She had given him a valuable gift without even knowing who he really was. A monster. He didn't deserve what she so willingly offered up. Nor did he deserve the dreamy look of trust and affection she was giving him now. Gabe wasn't sure if he wanted to laugh or cry so he went back to stroking her.

"It's early yet," he said, gaging the way the sun slanted through the window, "Let's go back to sleep."

They slept until late afternoon. Clouds had since darkened the sky and burst forth in a torrent of rain that pattered on the copper roof in a dull pitter-patter above them. Megan finally woke, loathe to leave the warmth of the man beside her. She got up slowly, slipping carefully from beneath his arm and put her bare feet down on the cold floor. She took the glass with its offensive odor and poured it down the sink before starting a pot of coffee. She closed the window silently and pulled a sketchpad and a charcoal pencil from the credenza and perched on the edge of the bed.

With careful strokes, Megan began creating his likeness. The hard lines of his muscular shoulders, the angle of his jaw, and his softly lidded eyes fringed with their thick lashes were all rendered expertly by her hand. She reached up and inched down the comforter to get a better view. She drew in a sharp breath as she revealed where the hard expanse of his abdomen tapered gracefully down his impressive shaft that stood at attention from within a thatch of thick black curls. She saw him stir for a moment and held her breath. Her heart beat wildly at the prospect of him waking to find her studying him but his breathing remained shallow so she continued her examination.

His member was generously and well proportioned. The perfect ratio of girth to length with a single vein running up the center to the smoothly rounded head. Megan blushed as she wondered how he had even managed to fit himself inside her. She felt a warmth pooling between her legs as she remembered exactly how well he filled her. As if they were made for one another. She tried to keep her objectivity as she pulled further on the fabric to reveal his powerful thighs and calves. She thought he had the most elegant shin bone that she had ever seen.

Sketch complete, Megan rewarded herself with a steaming cup of French vanilla with extra cream and sugar. She was admiring her own handiwork, figuring out how she would paint him when Gabe came up behind her.

"I don't think anyone has ever captured my image

like that before," he said and she startled, spilling some of the hot liquid on her.

"Good morning!" she said cheerily, face blazing.

"Good afternoon," he returned, looking at the clock.

"Want some coffee?" she enquired as she poured him a mug.

Gabe nodded.

She arched a brow at him, "How do you take it?"

He wasn't sure so he said, "Same as you is fine."

She handed him the mug and he inhaled the vanilla aroma before taking a sip. He closed his eyes and relish the flavor and warmth.

"Oh, that's good," he remarked aloud.

They shared the leftover apple crisp and spent the afternoon lounging around and chatting.

CHAPTER 10

The sound of the knocker startled him. Gabe ambled his way over to the carved double doors and flung them both wide.

"In here boys," he directed the youths and they wheeled the crates one by one into the great hall, mindful not to damage the marble floors with the dolly.

"Do you want us to set them up?" the one resembling a scarecrow asked.

Gabe put a long finger to the crease in his chin in thought before answering, "Go ahead and open the crates, please."

The shorter one pulled out a crowbar and set to work removing the boards.

"Carefully," he instructed them as they lifted out the newly framed canvases.

"You can lean them against that wall," he pointed to the closest one, "I'll hang them myself."

"You're sure? My boss said were to deliver, move, and hang the pieces," the young man said apprehensively.

"They're in good hands," Gabe assured them and handed each a hundred dollar bill.

Once the artwork was placed, the effect was uncanny. It was as if Gabe had added five new windows to the large room. He lay back against the blue silk pillows that adorned the enormous Tester bed to admire them. He pulled the slim cell from his pocket and dialed Megan.

"Are you awake?" he asked when she picked up.

"Hello, stranger. I was starting to think you'd never call," she rebuked, teasingly.

Megan had, in truth, experienced an inkling of worry when he had begged off of spending that Sunday with her. She knew it wasn't fair to judge him unkindly. It was underhanded of her to invite him to the Blarney Stone in the first place since it would essentially force him to meet her unconventional little family and it was probably too soon in their fledgling relationship for that.

"I take that as a yes, you're up," his deep voice rumbled in her ear.

She twirled a lock of hair around her finger like a schoolgirl, "Yes. Want to come over?" she asked with a blush.

Gabe had no doubts about what she had in mind if

the breathlessness invitation was any indication. His pants suddenly felt tighter and he closed his eyes for a moment, silently willing his erection to subside.

"Actually, I was thinking you could come have dinner here," he offered.

He found that he was feeling hesitant, and unsure once the invitation was put out there. He wanted her there but something about having her in his private space, answering her openly curious questions, unnerved him. Her shrewd emerald eyes didn't miss much and he didn't know if he could continue to lie to her and he was damned sure that if he told her the truth she'd run screaming into the night if she even believed him at all.

"That sounds great!"

She was so elated to have an opportunity to see this man she was falling for in his element that she almost forgot to ask, "Uh....Where do you live?"

"Do you know the old church on Main?" he asked.

"Of course. It's maybe a block and a half from here. Where do I go from there?" she had a pad out to write the directions.

"Nowhere," he answered.

"So you're meeting me at the church?" Megan assumed.

Gabe was standing on the granite steps awaiting her arrival.

When she saw him she launched into his arms and kissed him and when she settled down from her tiptoes she asked, "Where to?"

He smiled at her question, "Right here."

Megan's heart made an odd thud as she found herself wondering if he was homeless or was some sort of squatter.

"This is an old church," she stated the obvious.

He opened one of the large arched doors and held it wide.

"You coming?" he asked her, and she scurried up behind him.

Megan tried to take in the opulence of her surroundings. She felt like an imbecile for the train of her thoughts only moments before.

"Holy fucking shit!" she said, awestruck.

Gabe watched her face carefully. Her shrewd green eyes were taking in everything. Assessing every detail.

"I like it too," he said casually and walked over to one of the large damask settees. He patted the seat next to him.

"Do you want to come all the way in?"

She walked over, head in their air, admiring the way the chandeliers glowed against the golden wood that covered the entirety of the colossal vaulted ceiling and sat down. She looked at him as if for the first time and tried to think of something to say.

"It's incredible Gabe!" she exclaimed finally.

"I'm glad you like it," he smiled, pleased, and leaned over to kiss her.

Megan broke free from his lips.

"Can I have a tour?" she asked eagerly.

His laugh was a low rumble and his eyes twinkled blue, "Sure. After dinner."

The Risotto with Ossobuco was delicious. Megan raved about it to Gabe across the large dining table. He had really pulled out all the stops. She had loved the crystal cut bowl of autumnal roses and mums that adorned the center of the table and the large silver candlesticks with the softly glowing tapers dripping wax as they dined.

"I'm ready for that tour now," Megan said as she took the linen napkin from her lap and placed it on the table.

Gabe rose and pulled out her chair for her.

"Where do we start?" he began, "Well, this is the dining room although it's technically an aisle," he slowly as he spoke, letting her look her fill before moving on. "and this is the great hall which is, of course, the nave."

They had toured almost the entire downstairs. Gabe pointing out details along the way. When they had entered the kitchen, formerly the transept, Gabe was forced to confess that the dinner she enjoyed so well was really take-out Italian from Mamma Regina's and that Gabe did not cook. Megan hadn't missed the containers, nor the fact that the kitchen looked like it had never been used.

"So what's through there?" Megan asked curiously, pointing to a large door at the back of the kitchen.

"That's the sanctuary and the apse. Where they used to keep the altar and preform mass. I didn't think it was right to remodel it so I mostly use it for work," he told her.

Megan was touched and surprised by his reverence and mindfulness for the sacred space. She reached up and touched his face.

"Can I see it?" she asked.

"Maybe later. First I want to feed you dessert," he said and lifted her onto the cool granite countertop despite her squeals.

The shiny stainless refrigerator was empty save some baking soda, a couple bottles of wine, some creamer, and a white box. This he pulled out and placed on the long center island beside her.

"I wasn't sure what you'd like so I got a selection," he told her and lifted the lid.

Nestled among the fluted circles of paper were cannoli, neopolitans, tiramisu, tiny éclairs, rum balls and cream puffs.

"I love you," the words slipped from her mouth casually and they both stilled.

He took a cream puff from the box and placed it to her lips. She darted out a tongue to lick the whipped cream before taking a nip. His roman silver eyes never left hers. He took the pastry away and replaced it with his lips.

"Mm, tastes divine," he said and pulled her closer for another sample.

They climbed the winding stairs, side by side. Megan was dressed in nothing but Gabe's shirt, he in nothing but his jeans which he left unbuttoned. Even after being fulfilled so thoroughly on his kitchen counter, she couldn't help but experience the blood pooling in her loins as she admired him. The expanse of his broad, muscular shoulders, his well-formed pecs and washboard abs all tapered down to his not-too-narrow hips. The denim hung loosely there and she could see the dimpled top of his firm, round buttock as he walked in front of her. She admired it with due appreciation. It was dented at the sides and held the promise of power that had so far not disappointed.

"Holy shit!" Megan gawped once again, this time upon lifting her gaze from his butt and seeing his bedchamber.

Gabe confidently strode in and turned to her.

"I take it you like this room too?" he assumed.

Green eyes assessed every nuance from the antique Tester bedstead in the center of the room that was carved with cherubim to the high arched windows that ran from the floor to the top of the wall that vaulted to the frescoed ceiling. A midnight and gold oriental covered most of the glossy walnut floors. Facing the curtained bed was a rose window. The geometrical pattern of stained glass panes layering different shapes upon one another until they formed a perfect circle.

"It's incredibly beautiful," she whispered reverently.

"You should see it in daylight."

He was glad she had enough sense to appreciate what was to him, the most important part of the room, possibly the entire building.

"Do you like how I placed your paintings?" he asked.

She was reluctant to tear her gaze from the masterpiece before her but turned her attention to the space below. So drawn to the window, Megan hadn't even noticed them there.

The five canvases hung in a row, creating more windows on the stone wall. He had placed them in a certain order that Megan herself hadn't even contemplated. First came Nightwatch, then Night's Edge. Next was City Rising followed by Daydream and Daybreak and last was Sleeping City. She couldn't help but marvel at the way that they seemed to depict a perfect revolution of the sun.

Gabe put his arms around her as two hot tears traced twin paths from her eyes to her chin. She wasn't sure what had brought on the waterworks. Perhaps it was the thoughtfulness of the man who held her. The man who seemed to understand her in a way that she didn't even understand herself.

"You can't possibly know what this means to me," she said as she turned in his arms and pulled him down for a kiss.

He lifted her in his arms and carried to the bed like a precious gift. He laid her down carefully on the luxurious bedding and made love to her slowly until the sun rose.

CHAPTER 11

Megan woke to an empty space beside her. She slid off the satin sheets, her feet touching the soft silk of the carpet. It was dark save for the first rays of morning filtering in through the long windows, casting all in a bluish tinge. She noticed that one of the windows on the wall opened into the night. She carefully picked her way through the dim room to it and peeked her head out cautiously.

Gabe was standing on one of the buttresses staring off into the dawn. The sun was just edging over the horizon. She was going to step out to join him but something stopped her. She simply watched in breathless wonder the stillness and beauty of him as the first golden rays touched his skin, making him a gilded statue of some ageless god from an era long past. Her fingers itched to paint him. To create a venerated icon of this man whom she knew so little but to whom she was enthralled. Megan realized at that moment that he had her heart. She was deeply and irrevocably in love with him and that realization made her heart soar.

The couple spent the next days entirely in each other's company. They spent their days in bed making love or napping and their nights in restaurants and nightclubs or the theatre.

Gabe was treating Megan like a princess and for the first time she was enjoying having a boyfriend to hold hands with as they crossed the street or to make out with during a movie. She hadn't even been back to her apartment for more than a change of clothes since the first night she was there. She discovered, much to her delight, that Gabe fit nicely in the claw-foot tub although the shower at his place was much bigger and more practical for them to bathe each other in as they began making a habit of.

Megan had made herself at home with him and she relished falling asleep in his arms and waking to sketch him before he woke or as he leaned against the balustrade while he thought she slept.

Megan had almost been with him a week when she woke up from a dream with a strange thought in her head. She slid out of the blankets and threw on Gabe's shirt and went over to the wall. It was there that she began studying a spot on one of the paintings.

Gabe came up behind her and put his hands on her slim shoulders.

"Geez, you scared me, Gabe. I almost had a heart attack!" she said startled.

It was dawn and she had expected Gabe to be outside watching the sun rise.

He laughed and apologized then noticed where her attention had been riveted so intently that she hadn't heard him approach.

"What are we looking at?" he asked.

Megan pointed to the spot on *Nightwatch* where the figure of a man was leaning on the very point he stood only moments before.

"That's you!" she pointed.

Gabe leaned in and inspected the painting and a brow rose.

"So it is," he said, seeming nonplussed.

"That's odd. I wonder if since I can see you from my place you'd be able to see me as well," she mused.

He shifted uncomfortably and she turned to eye him suspiciously. He flinched so slightly from her gaze that anyone beside her probably wouldn't have noticed.

"Can you see my place from there, Gabe?" she asked directly.

He averted the green fire of her stare. She put her hands on her slim waist, waiting. He didn't answer her. The thought that was nagging at the back of her brain was now seeming to take form.

Megan walked over to the window and climbed out onto the buttress. What she found when she reached the spot he was standing chilled her to the bone. Propped near one of the gargoyles was a slim pair of binoculars. She picked them up and brought them inside with her, remaining deadly silent. She put them down on the bed and started dressing, her whole body shaking.

"Megan…" he began but she ignored him.

She wanted his excuses too much to allow herself to hear them. She took her shoes in her hand and made her way down the stairs in a huff. She was in such a state that she could barely remember her way around the gigantic building in the gloom. As if guided by instinct she spotted the front door from which she'd entered. Her purse and coat were hanging on a rack beside it. She practically ran across the large room to recover them stopping only to recover a dropped heel as she fumbled to grab her belongings.

"Megan wait!" Gabe called from the stairs, "Let me explain!"

Megan whipped her head around before the tears that were threatening to fall would spill for him to see. She opened the door and walked out without turning back.

CHAPTER 12

"Thank you, ma'am," the man behind the desk said.

He handed Megan back the untidy stack of papers along with her I.D. card and her new passport. She turned to her mother who was stowing a worn romance into her purse as she rose from the blue plastic chair and stretched.

"All set then, Love?" Josephine asked.

Megan pushed open the glass door.

"All set. Are you sure you won't come with?" she asked her for what could've been the hundredth time, hoping the answer had changed.

"You'll do fine, Megs. Besides, ya know it'll take me too long to renew my own passport. The only reason ya got one so fast was because of the letter from the lawyer and the documents about yer father," she reminded her.

To Megan, hearing any mention of her father was still strange.

"I know, Ma," she admitted reluctantly.

It, in fact, wasn't as speedy a process as Megan had hoped. She was grateful to Gayle for making her apply as soon as she showed her the letter and the tickets. It had taken two weeks before she got the email informing her that her passport was ready.

"Ya sure two days isn't too soon for ya ta be leavin'?" the concern was apparent in Josephine's husky voice.

"I'm sure, Ma, It'll only be gone for a week or two and I have nothing else going on in my life right now."

She tried really hard to not think about Gabe or the reason for her need to put an entire ocean between them.

"Let's go get some lunch and go shopping. I still need some things for the trip," she said as she took the other woman's hand and led her with what she had hoped appeared as enthusiasm, to the subway.

Megan stood on a ladder hanging her newly purchased black drapes. They hung from ceiling to floor in a cascade of thick velvet that the saleswoman assured her would block out any prying eyes. She had paid a pretty penny for them and found that comfort they would bring her would be worth it.

She spent the rest of the day packing everything she would need into the new suitcase she had purchased with her mother. She felt hollow.

She tore tags off sweaters, shirts, and underwear and stuffed them inside the big bag along with old and faded jeans and heavy knit socks. Josephine had also insisted she pack a couple of dresses and heels even though she assured her she wouldn't need them but the woman insisted and finally Megan relented.

She packed her carryon separate. In that went the things she couldn't live without. Pencils, sketchpads, Oreos, comfortable clothes and her nightgown. She packed a toothbrush, hairbrush, and lipstick in a cosmetic case that she tucked inside. She wouldn't be able to bring any soaps or other liquid toiletries without having to deal with airport security so the plan was to buy them when she arrived and hoped that they had her brand of toothpaste in Ireland.

Once the packing was finished, Megan ordered enough Chinese food to feed an army although she wasn't expecting any guests. She and Gayle had already said their goodbyes the previous night and her, Ham and her mother that afternoon. She knew that eating away her problems wasn't the best strategy but she wasn't a drinker and having a wall of black fabric was a painful reminder of what she was trying to block out. No amount of eggrolls wouldn't fill the void she felt in the vicinity of her heart but they did help dull the pit of hot despair that was eating away the lining of her stomach.

The takeoff was long and uneventful aside from Megan gripping her armrest tightly with her sweaty palms. The view was incredible but every bit of turbulence seemed to mirror her inner turmoil and send waves of anxiety through her entire body until it found its way out of her by way of slick perspiration.

Halfway through the flight, she had relaxed enough to enjoy the novelty of the experience of flying for the first time and the added bonus of it being first class. She gave credit for her change in mood to the flight attendant who had brought her a complimentary glass of wine without her asking and insisting she'd enjoy it and that it would calm her. The white was cool and fragrant and relaxed her tattered nerves.

Hot canapés were served and the knot in Megan's stomach dissipated completely and she found she was quite enjoying herself. She was being served a five star meal on Wedgewood china while flying through the air across the Atlantic in a metal bird. It was magical. She realized she'd be a fool to even think of home and all that transpired there or even what awaited her in the foreign land she was on her way to. There would be nothing beside the now and she was determined to live in the moment. She sucked down as many free cokes with extra cherries as she could and ordered a fruit and cheese plate and a large slice of chocolate ganache cake and rode the sugar high right into Dublin airport.

The two hour bus ride through the Irish countryside was breathtaking. She was glad she had opted for her chosen mode of transport instead of calling the car service as the lawyer had instructed her on the phone when she dialed him from the airport.

They drove through the city and the suburbs and out into miles of rolling green hills. Megan sketched everything from her fellow passengers to the landscape, feeling at peace. She idly wondered if the freedom she felt from being a stranger in a strange land was why so many people she knew in college spent their summers backpacking through Europe. *Did her mother feel like this?*

Thoughts of her mother brought Megan back to the place she was heading. She was forced to remind herself that she wasn't on vacation. At least not yet. She intended to see through her date with the attorney and do her part, but after that, she wanted to take advantage of the free trip once the business part was over.

"Ms. Black! Pleased to meet ya! Top o' the mornin'!" the little man pumped her hand vigorously, "Come sit down! Please," he eagerly bade her and Megan took a seat in the armchair across from the tidy desk before Mr. McCredie plopped his wide bottom down on the leather wingchair behind it. "So, ya took the bus, did ya?" his blue eyes twinkled mischievously.

"Yes, sorry. I wanted to see the countryside and a car service is not really my thing," she apologized.

He waved a pudgy hand in admonishment, "Quite alright Ms. Black. A little stodgy for me too."

Megan couldn't help but like the squat, smiling attorney. She laughed openly at his conspiratorial comment.

"How'd ya like the room?" he asked her.

"It was really nice," she said honestly.

The bed and breakfast in which Mr. McCredie had

booked her lodgings was a tribute to toile but Megan found that the food was delicious and the woman who ran it, Mrs. McDonough, was a pleasant blue-haired woman who loved to gossip.

"Jeff Donovan will be there in ten minutes," a female voice over the intercom announced.

"Brilliant, Claire. Can you fetch Miss Black and me 'self a coffee please while we're waitin'?" he asked and hit the button.

"Who's Jeff Donovan?" Megan asked as Claire, the assistant who had ushered her in to the office, poured out the steaming brown liquid into teacups.

Mr. McCredie waited until the thin blonde shut the door behind her before answering, "Mr. Donovan would be a cousin o' yours. He wasn't listed in yer father's will but he wanted ta be here for the readin' of it. Called me after the good Reverend passed sayin' he was the next of kin and his only livin' heir. I was forced to inform him of yer existence and yer claim. He didn't seem too happy about that, I'll tell ya."

Megan wanted to ask more questions but Claire's voice cut through the conversation once more, "Mr. Donovan's here."

Mr. McCredie's stubby finger hit the button, "Thank

ya, Claire. Send him in."

A tall man with neatly clipped brown hair entered the room. The attorney rose from his seat and leaned over his desk to shake the other man's hand.

"Mr. Donovan," he said by way of greeting in a much more reserved tone than he had used with her.

"Mr. McCredie," he said formally as he clasped the proffered and shook it.

"This would be yer cousin Miss Megan Black.," he introduced her to the standing man beside her. He looked maybe thirty-something. His suit was expensive but it looked like it had seen better days

The man eyed her suspiciously for a moment, his hazel eyes appraising her features. She had her mother's bone structure and creamy skin, and her grandfather's black hair but she did have one attribute that was undeniably Johnathan Lucas Donovan. His eyes.

He must've made the decision that they truly were relations because he reached out his hand to her, "Jeff Donovan," he said.

"Nice to meet you," she said as she took his palm in hers. It was hot and moist and she couldn't wait to drop it and covertly wipe her leg on her pants. She had a strong dislike for men who had smooth hands as if they never did an honest day's work in their lives. Even the attorney had roughened calluses on his palms.

"Have a seat Mr. Donovan and I'll call in Claire so we can get started," he instructed and hit the call button once more.

Mr. McCredie hadn't offered any coffee to the man and she wondered why he appeared to dislike him. To her, he seemed harmless if harried.

The reading of the will was long and tedious and Megan regretted accepting the coffee. Her bladder was full and she thought it would be rude to excuse herself to use the restroom. She crossed her legs instead and sat back in the chair and tried to concentrate on the words being spoken. The lawyer had already listed off what would remain the property of the church and what would go to charity when he finally mentioned her name.

"My daughter Megan Black, will receive the rest of my estate including my journals, books, art collection, personal effects not already mentioned above, and the entirety of my trust which will immediately be made available to her upon my demise," he read.

"Is there anything else?" Jeff Donovan asked him. "Anything about me?"

"Sorry, no. Reverend Donovan was very specific in his will. I helped him draft it me 'self. Megan is his sole heir. Now if you'll excuse us, I have some paperwork I need Miss Black's signature on and we need to go over some other details," it was a dismissal.

The tall man's face darkened, "He was my uncle. Until he died, I wasn't even aware that this 'daughter'," the word daughter was said distastefully, "even existed!"

The lawyer folded his palms over his rotund belly and sat back casually.

"It doesn't matter if you had knowledge of her, Mr. Donovan. Her father did. He went to great lengths to find her and to assure that she was taken care of."

"How do we even know she is who she says she is?" he asked belligerently.

"Show him your passport if you wish Miss Black," the little man suggested calmly.

Jeff Donovan's face turned an ugly shade of red as he spluttered, "I meant how you know she's even his real daughter and not just some imposter trying to make a buck? Has he had a DNA test done? Who is her mother? How did they meet?" he asked all of these in quick succession and the lawyer's face remained placid.

"That's none of your affair, Mr. Donovan. The will

is a binding legal contract and I am just the attorney who was hired to read it and see it executed. Now if you'll excuse us," he dismissed him again.

"No, I won't excuse you!" he yelled down, "I demand some type of recourse! I'm not sure how you country people handle your laws but I assure you that I will be contacting my own attorney back in the States and you'd both better watch your backs!"

"Is that a threat Mr. Donovan?" Mr. McCredie asked him quizzically.

He seemed like he was completely at ease with someone screaming in his face because Megan saw him smile ever so slightly and the twinkle in his eye was back.

"It's a promise," the other man warned.

Jeff Donovan was obviously the type who was used to getting his way either through his sense of entitlement or by outright bullying. The attorney seemed to have reached the limit of his patience.

He stood and met the irate man's gaze head on and boomed, "I've had enough of ya sullyin' my office and upsetting my invited guest," he shot Megan a quick wink, "Now shove off with ya! Go call yer lawyer in the States because if ya think yer goin' ta sit and my office and threaten me or Miss Black yer goin ta need him because I'm goin' ta see ya thrown in jail!"

The demeanor of the stout man had completely changed from pussycat to ferocious lion and Megan could picture him in a courthouse in front of a judge tearing a witness to shreds on the stand.

The taller man was the first to back down. Megan stifled a giggle as he grabbed his coat off the chair in a huff just as Claire opened the door for him to walk out.

"Good riddance," said the blonde woman, "That man was a terrible arsehole."

Megan laughed at the epithet and the tension leeched from the office.

Megan used the bathroom and upon her return, she felt much better. They set to work immediately. She signed paper after paper first conceding that she was the sole and rightful heir and second designating her as the recipient of the trust fund.

"You didn't ask how much it was for," Mr. McCredie noted as she initialed the last document.

"Oh. Should I?" she asked lamely.

He eyed her speculatively then answered, "Twenty seven million three hundred thousand and forty-four. American."

Megan collapsed back into her chair.

"Holy fucking shit!" she said out loud.

"Quite."

He pulled a bottle and two glasses from his desk drawer and poured two fingers each.

"I can't drink whiskey," she admitted.

"Good thing its bourbon then, lass. Cheers," he said and picked up his glass.

"Cheers," she echoed and saluted with her glass.

The dark amber liquid burned a trail of fire down her throat and settled in her stomach in a pool of warmth. Her nerves calmed instantly.

"So where did a man of the cloth come up with so much scratch?" she wondered out loud.

"Yer grandparents. Yer Da was what you Americans call a trust fund baby. The whole lot of 'em born with silver spoons, mind ya," he waved his glass animatedly as he spoke, "it seemed yer Da had a higher callin'. He set out ta be a priest. Your grand da didn't like it much, his son not takin' to the family business, but let him have his way.

He was a smart man, yer grandfather. He put certain provisions on yer Da's trust fund so that yer father couldn't touch it unless he met certain requirements. In that way, Luke wouldn't be able ta just give all of it away ta either the church or charity. That would be nonsense, o' course, but like I said earlier; yer grandfather was a very smart man. I can see yer Da usin' it to help others in need. The older Mr. Donovan wasn't a complete bumbler, though. He didn't want ta hurt his son fer choosing the holy life so he made sure ta donate in his name and ta give him an allowance that he could do with what he chose."

Megan was about to open her mouth to ask a question but she knew better than to interrupt and Irishman while in the middle of a story.

"When yer grandfather passed away some ten years ago, yer Da's trust became his ta manage along with his portion of the inheritance from his father. Seems this caused a stir with Luke's older brother William, who I'm sure has pissed through the last o' what he got by now. Bloody imbecile. That would be yer cousin's father.

At the time William thought he was entitled to your Da's share of the money plus his own and tried all means ta get his grubby fingers on it. William's son is just like the old coot, as ya probably could tell."

He was talking about Jeff and Megan could definitely see the greed and sense of superiority in the man.

McCredie let her digest some of his words before picking up where he left off, "I was already your Da's attorney by then, plus Luke and I were friends."

Her eyebrow rose like a crow's wing and Megan started to ask, "Where...?"

"Where do you come in, ya wonder?" he asked suddenly. Intuiting her thoughts before the words fully formed.

She nodded.

"Weel, that's the beginning o' the story. Likely, I should've started there," he clasped his hands over the top of his round belly.

"Your Da came back ta Ireland some twenty five years or so looking fer a Josephine Black but none o' the locals would talk ta him so he came and found me. I wasn't in these offices, mind. I was workin' out o' a hole in the wall with cheap paneling and a stained shag rug in Galway city with nothin' more than a couple folding chairs and the desk from my room back home. I had just passed the board and was green, mind, but I was willin' ta hear the man out. Seems yer Da was feelin' guilty and came back ta find your Ma and marry her. He was willing ta leave the priesthood behind fer the lass if she couldn't abandon her Catholic faith and become the wife o' a Protestant but he couldn't find her and no one was talking. They acted as if she never existed.

At any rate, he offered me a ridiculous sum ta track her down but she had left Ireland altogether. He waited a full year here in Galway fer her return but she never came back. He took it as a sign from God ta continue in his service and he did. He took up a position in Clifden and was content there ta serve," he paused long enough to top of their glasses.

Megan carefully nursed her own drink, appreciating the scent that made her think of a quiet winter evening before a fire in a fine leather armchair eating a toasted vanilla cookie that had been drizzled with caramel and topped with a cherry, except for the heat of the fire roared inside her with each tiny sip. Its heat melting away all worries and cares and she found herself relaxed as she listened to the musical lilt of the man who sat across from her weaving a web of intrigue.

"It took about four years before I finally located yer mother," he continued, "she didn't wish ta speak ta me and returned many o' my letters unopened and didn't answer my calls. I hired out a private investigator ta check in on her. See what she was doing. See if she was happy. I thought maybe it would give yer Da some peace, ya understand."

"Of course," Megan mumbled.

He savored a swallow of the liquor as if he'd need it for what came next in his tale, "I wasn't shocked ta hear from him saying as how yer mother was livin' in Boston with a big hulk o' a man or that she had a child. These things happen ya know," as if summing up the way of the world, "Anyway, I thought nothin' o' it at all until the detective sent me the pictures he had taken of you with yer Ma."

He looked different. As if he had left the office and had gone back in time.

"You have Luke's eyes," he told her before continuing, "I wasn't sure what ta do from there. Did I present my good friend with the fantastic news that the lass was living well and happy or did I tell him that there was a distinct possibility that he had a child who was being raised by another man and break his heart?"

"What did you do?" Megan asked, enrapt. It was as if this story was about some fictional character and not her at all.

"I'll tell you what I didn't do lass. I didn't tell Luke anythin'. I'm sorry. I know I've been a blighter and you have every right ta be angry with me," his head sunk down in misery and Megan almost felt sorry for him. Mr. McCredie did really seem like a likeable fellow who wanted to do the right thing in a hard situation.

"So how was it that I came to be written in the will if he didn't know I existed?" she asked suspiciously, eyeing him over the rim of the cut glass tumbler.

The lawyer looked like he was glad she asked, "Well when yer father got sick he came to me askin' about yer mother and if I'd ever found anything. Seems he hadn't forgotten but maybe gave up. I couldn't keep it from him any longer. Twasn't right. He deserved ta have the truth o' it so I showed him the pictures. I thought he'd be angry or crushed but instead he was happy. The happiest I'd ever seen him. Surely, he was regretful o' the time lost but he was so pleased ta know he had a daughter out there. He asked me ta send out another investigator ta check up on you and find anything he could. What you were like, yer grades in school, yer growing up, boyfriends. Everytin'. Then he rewrote his will for you. He may not have been able to be there because he didn't want to disturb yer life selfishly, but knowing you were his made his last days his gladdest. He went ta God a happy man."

Megan began sobbing uncontrollably and Mr. McCredie came around from the desk to sooth her.

"There, lass, there now," he cooed as she bawled all over his tweed jacket.

"I'm s-sorry," she cried, "I th-think I'm probably j-just drunk," she said as she tried to stop the spasms that came from trying to force her grief back inside.

"It's okay Megan. Maybe I should take ya over ta Mrs. McDonough's though she'll probably wag her tongue all over plus your cousin Jeff is there, bloody idiot," he seemed to be trying to work out what to do.

After thinking for a moment he said, "I know. You can stay at the vicarage. You'd have ta be there anyway ta go through your Da's things. Yes, I have the key right here and yer to have full access anyway. This is best."

"Okay," Megan agreed, drying her eyes on the sleeve of her sweater.

He father really loved her, Megan thought. He loved her enough to stay away for fear of disrupting her life. That kind of selflessness couldn't have come easy. Yes, things could've been easier in her life if she had a father but she had Ham to play that role and upon thinking on it, she decided that she wouldn't have changed anything. Her trials and struggles made her the person she was.

She mulled over that lovely thought as Mr. McCredie's car zoomed along the streets and over hills until they arrived at what had once been her father's former residence standing about a quarter mile from the massive church that he also had called home.

She had thanked Mr. McCredie and he had given her another of his business cards and a keyring with at least a dozen keys on it and wished her well and waited until she had gotten inside and found the light before pulling away into the blackness.

Megan had far too much to think about to sleep and the vicarage was too old and beautiful not to explore. She was surprised when she arrived to see the how large the house she'd be staying in was. It was an impressive manner built not too far from the church proper and boasted at least twenty rooms. It was comfortably furnished with antiques that had probably stayed behind after each of the inhabitants finished their posts. Megan was delighted by the number of books in the library and the quality of the art that hung on the wall. It was mostly landscapes of the countryside and churchyard with a few excellently rendered portraits, almost all signed J.L.D. Megan was awed at finding out who she'd gotten her talent from. It felt strange as so much else about this trip and even the last month leading up to it had.

She had made herself a cup of tea and carried it with her on her expedition. She found what must have been her late father's office and sat down behind his desk. There was a stain in the shape of a ring so she placed her cup and saucer in that spot and wondered about what her father must've been like. She glanced through the papers on the cluttered blotter and rifled through the drawers. The one on the bottom right was locked and Megan wondered if the key was amongst the set that Peter McCredie had given her before he departed. She went to fetch them to find out.

After going through the entire ring to find a key of suitable size, Megan tried the lock. The drawer opened and inside she found a stack of leather bound journals. She pulled them out and placed them reverently on the desktop. She stared at them for a while, wondering if she should read them. It seemed like such an invasion of privacy despite the fact that they were specifically awarded to her in the will. Finally, her need to understand the man that was her father superseded her misgivings and she cracked the cover of the one on the top.

January.1st,
2011

Today starts a new year although I probably won't live to see the end of it. The good doctor told me I didn't have much longer. I felt so sorry for the poor woman to have to give me the news. I could see the sorrow and compassion in her eyes. I wished she knew that I wasn't afraid and that the Good Lord will take me at the time he feels best as he does with us all. I will go to the gates of Saint Peter knowing I have lived a full life of goodness and purpose.

Tears began to spring to her eyes so Megan skipped forward to a later entry.

May 6th,
2012

The mysteries of our world astound me. What had been my greatest sin and the deepest wound has turned into a mighty blessing. Peter has given me a gift in the form of a miracle. He has, after all of these long years, found my Josephine. I know she is no longer mine if ever she was, but to know that she is well and still using her gifts is a boon to my heart. That knowledge itself would've been enough for me to go in peace but it seemed my old friend had so much more to offer.

I find myself marveling at His will for He has kept me alive not only so I could learn of my lost love but that I am a father! I have a beautiful daughter who has just graduated college. I am bursting with pride and wish that I could be there to share in such an auspicious occasion. I know such a thing is not prudent or possible so instead, I will pray that God sends her an angel in my stead.

A picture was taped to the top the next page. It was of a three or four year old girl with pigtails wearing a pink dress. She band aids on both of her knees. It was Megan. She was holding her mother's hand in front of the Blarney Stone and in the other hand, she held a stuffed panda with the tag still hanging from it. She pulled the photo free to examine it.

Megan remembered that day vividly. It was her first trip to the zoo and Uncle Ham had filled her up with so much popcorn and ice cream and cotton candy that she threw up all over his shoes in the monkey house. Her mother had scolded her and they had to leave early so Ham could clean up. It was one of Megan's first memories. The photograph had to have been snapped from across the street, judging from the perspective, and she wondered who had taken it.

She slid the photograph back between the pages. Her index finger came back bleeding from a paper cut. It stung but no worse than reading the journal had. She put it in her mouth and sucked on it and went to find her bed so that she could cry herself to sleep.

CHAPTER 13

The sound of church bells woke Megan from her dreamless slumber. She crept through the large house to the kitchen and was grateful to find a French press and some coffee beans in a cabinet. The thought of tea in the morning offended her American sensibilities and she was glad her father had obviously felt the same. She searched the cupboards for a grinder and set to work filling a kettle and grinding the beans. Megan poured the steaming water from the kettle into the carafe and pressed down. The refrigerator had been emptied so she was forced to take it black. She heaped in extra spoonfuls of sugar to make up for the lack of cream.

She took a few gulps that burned her tongue, then took the steaming mug into the light filled office and took up her previous seat behind the desk. She knew she wasn't ready yet to dive back into the journals quite yet so instead she enjoyed her coffee and searched for other treasures.

There was a lovely book of poetry that she decided she'd take and a first edition Moby Dick that had the initials J.L.D. on the inside corner of the cover. She rummaged through more furniture and inside a credenza she found a stack of unopened letters addressed bearing her mother's name. She set them with her other findings. She wasn't sure if she wanted to open those or not.

When the pot of coffee was gone and the entire room gone through, Megan's stomach began to protest loudly.

"I know. I need to eat something before I pass out," she told the complaining body part in hopes that it would quiet down.

She dressed quickly in jeans and boots and her hoodie. She grabbed the keys and her bag and stepped out the door, locking it behind her, intent on walking into town in search of breakfast.

A few people waved curiously as they drove past her on the road and she returned their greeting with a smile.

It was only a quarter of a mile before she hit the main street of the small village. Her mood was fine until she was slammed with a sudden panic when she realized there weren't any restaurants around. She pulled out her phone and dialed the personal number the lawyer had given her.

"Mr. McCredie?" she asked when he picked up.

"Megan! Top o' the morning! I hope you found yer stay well."

"Yes. Thank you," she answered automatically.

"Brilliant! Now, what can I do for you, my girl?" he asked.

Megan felt oddly embarrassed, "I was just wondering if there's any restaurants or places to eat in Clifden."

"Quite right. You'll be wantin' breakfast fer sure. I forgot to think of it as the plans had you at the inn. Let me think," he said and went quiet.

She heard him talking to someone she realized was his assistant Claire in the background before he came back on. She hadn't realized the two were an item the previous day.

"Megan, there's another inn on the main street across from the pub. You can get lunch at either. There's a bakery that serves coffee and the like over on Market. Claire says to go to the castle for dinner. And Megan?" her savior asked.

"Yes, Mr. McCredie," she responded.

"Next time use your Da's car. The keys are on the ring and it's parked in the carriage house. It has GPS. I don't want ya havin' ta walk everywhere. There's a lot o' space out there on the roads and people may not be used ta pedestrians that early," he warned.

"Thanks, Mr. McCredie," she said.

"It's Peter. Or even Uncle Peter," he offered her.

"Thanks, Uncle Peter," she said, liking the familiarity and hung up.

Megan brought what was left of the spoils of her outing back to the vicarage with her. She'd bought way too much but she didn't want to have to go out every morning, not after that walk. Her legs burned from overuse and her shoulders ached from the hour long trek with the totes. They definitely didn't seem that heavy when she had first set off.

She put the box of scones on the kitchen table and emptied the paper bag of sundries next to it. She unloaded the cream and the eggs into the fridge along with some milk and sandwich meats. She left the bread out on the counter with a small jar of mayonnaise and some homemade pickles that caught her fancy in the little market. She didn't bother unpacking the toiletries as those would go into the bathroom on her way upstairs.

Once all that was taken care of Megan was bored. She took her phone out of her back pocket and dialed her mother.

"Meg? Is everytin' alright?" her mother answered, startled.

"Everything's fine, mom," she assured her.

"It's the middle o' the bloody night! Jesus, I'd thought sometin' was the matter," she sounded tired.

"I'm sorry Ma, I forgot about the time difference. Go back to sleep," she said and ended the call.

Megan wasn't sure what to do so she went back to exploring before finding herself back in the big red leather chair behind the Reverend's desk again. She flipped opened a different journal than the one she had been reading the previous night and found that it contained mostly empty pages. She flipped backward until she found an entry.

August 28th,
2014

Today is my last day. I can feel it. I am so very tired. I can hear the angels calling me home and I do not think I can ignore them any longer. Their music sounds so peaceful and yet I find myself suddenly afraid. Not for myself but for my daughter. I worry that she will live her life alone without the joy of love to warm her heart. I at least have her and my memories of Josephine to take with me and the love of the Lord to fill my heart but she has no one of her own. The possibility that my absence has somehow contributed to her closing herself off weighs heavily on me.

I prayed again last night and again this morning for an angel to be sent her way. I'm sure an angel can open her heart. I already know the one who has been watching over her in my stead, though I'm certain he doesn't know that he is one. The funny thing about dying is that you can see things as if from the other side. It is a curious thing to see angels walking among us. I know I must sound mad. Maybe I am. The

mad ramblings of a dying man.

Megan was becoming accustomed to the tears that fell at her father's words. That last entry was extremely hard for her to get through. She wondered if there was truth to them or if they were simply the musings of a very ill man of very strong faith. *Was she really closed off to love?*

She allowed her thoughts to linger on Gabe for the first time since her take-off from Logan. She had opened her heart to him and he had stabbed her in it with his deception. She admitted to herself, in fairness, that she had been a fool to not ask him questions. Not to push for answers when she noticed him evading her. The red flags were there but she had ignored them all. It was just as much her fault as anyone else's and that realization made her bitter.

She decided to make a list of what she did know about Gabe on one of her father's notepads and found it painfully short. She knew where he lived but not how he made a living. She knew what his skin felt like and how he tasted and that he couldn't cook but he could dance. She knew he didn't sleep much and that he was always there when she needed him. *Probably because he was watching me*, she reminded herself bitterly. The thought stuck with her, though. Why was he watching her? Could he have been the P.I. hired to keep tabs on her? Megan pulled out her phone and dialed Peter McCredie.

"Uncle Peter, this is Megan. I had a question. What was the name of the private investigator you hired?" she hit the pound key signaling her message was complete. She was disappointed that she'd have to wait for his answer.

Megan drove cautiously down the winding and aptly named Sky Road that led to the castle as the sky turned pink and reflected of the ocean in a dazzling display. She wasn't used to driving and having to do it on the left side proved to be more difficult than she imagined. Luckily for her, traffic was light and a valet that had been standing attention came out and took the car when she pulled onto the enormous flagstone drive.

It had taken Megan some time to deduce which castle she was supposed to dine in. She had tried to look it up on her smartphone and found that the entire area was dotted with the large stone structures, some ruins and others rebuilt. She had taken a chance when choosing the name of the largest one though it was much newer than the rest of the castles and wasn't in Clifden proper.

She sent out a prayer of thanks to her mother for insisting she pack a dress as she was ushered into the posh yet intimate dining room. Enormous crystal chandeliers hung from the cavernous vaulted ceiling. And the flagstone fireplace was big enough to park a car in.

Someone pulled out a chair for Megan and she sat down and put her crisp white napkin in her lap. A waiter came and poured her a glass of champagne and handed her a menu. Everything looked delicious. Megan was torn between sampling the seafood and getting the rack of lamb. She opted for the lamb since it seemed to be a specialty. The waiter told her it was a "Good choice." And marched off.

Megan sipped the champagne, letting the bubbles tickle her nose while she waited for her dinner. Couples filled most of the tables and Megan sighed, wondering if she was destined to be alone as her father had feared. She remembered what it was like to sit across from Gabe having dinner and conversation. She missed him and it wasn't just the companionship but the way he made her feel like the only woman on earth. Like every word uttered from her lips was vital to him.

The road was dark and slick and Megan was careful as she navigated her way back to the manse that held what was left of her father. From a distance, she could see that the lights were on inside. Megan couldn't remember if she turned them on or not but it didn't seem like her to be so wasteful. An uneasy feeling crept up her spine as she pulled into the carriage-house and cut the engine.

Megan went to fetch the can of pepper spray from her purse just in case but she came up empty handed. Weapons of any sort weren't allowed on airplanes and she most definitely wasn't in Boston anymore. She grabbed the key ring instead, arranging the keys so that one poked out between her index and middle finger and the rest clenched in her closed fist before walking to the door. It was unlocked and a shiver of fear ran up her spine.

Her heart pounded in her chest as she stepped inside. She was trying to convince herself that she had just been careless and forgot to lock up and shut the lights. She heard a noise from the study and almost jumped out of her skin. She clenched her fisted hand tightly and tiptoed up to the door and peered inside.

Jeff Donovan was rifling through the desk and

cursing to himself. Megan decided to go back outside and call the police. She took four steps backward before the floor creaked. She stood frozen, listening to see if the noise was registered. It was hard to hear over her pulse roaring in her ears and her choppy breathing. After what felt like an eternity, Megan took another step back. Then another. She turned to make her way back to the door.

"Going somewhere?" Jeff asked from behind her as she turned to face the door.

"Yes, actually I am," she answered tartly, covering her shock at him appearing at her back so quickly.

He moved and blocked her path. She tried to sidestep him.

"I don't think so Miss Black," he warned, his face a mask of hatred.

If he wouldn't let her pass by him she'd have to go through him.

"Move!" she shouted and barreled into him enough, pushing him on her way toward the door.

He grabbed her arm viciously and yanked her toward him. She still had the key in her enclosed fist and shot out a quick jab to his temple, just as Uncle Ham had shown her. She had only nicked him but he reeled back in pain and blood spattered on the wide pine floors.

Megan used the opening to dart from the house. She
fumbled in her bag for her cell, cursing herself for
carrying the large bag, as she made her way back to the
graveled drive and relative safety. She dialed nine-one-
one but nothing happened.

"Shit," she muttered in exasperation.

She couldn't recall the international equivalent. She
tried to look it up on the internet with shaking hands.
Suddenly the wind was knocked out of her and she was
on the ground, the phone out of reach.

"I told you you'd pay you little bitch," he screeched
in her ear.

Megan struggled against him, trying to connect her
knee with his groin. Jeff Donovan may have been a
spoiled rich kid but he was strong. Megan knew she had
to think quickly and clearly. She could hear Ham's voice,
"Never be angry in a fight, Megs. Ya can't think clearly
if yer angry. Ya need to keep a level head if ya hope ta
win."

"Sierra!" she called to her phone, "Call McCredie!

"Calling McCredie," she heard the robotic voice say.

Jeff said, "I don't think so!" and lunged for the
phone. She scrambled to get up as he smashed her phone
against the gravel and brought his heel down hard,

ruining her hopes of communicating with the outside world.

"Now, what am I going to do with you?" he asked darkly but he didn't give her time to answer. His fist came down and her vision went dark.

CHAPTER 14

Megan came to in her father's office. Her hands and legs were bound to a chair with duct tape. There was a matching piece across her mouth and it was hard for her to suck in the ragged gasps of air through her nose. She thought she might pass out again and tried to slow her breathing. Her head pounded. She did a quick internal survey. She was bruised and battered but she didn't think she was bleeding. That fact alone calmed her.

"Glad to see you're awake," Jeff said from somewhere in the room. She craned her neck as far as she could until she spotted him in her father's chair, his fingers steepled together on the desk. She couldn't help but notice the phone not even inches from her arm.

He must've seen her look of longing because he smiled and said, "I don't think so. No one is coming to help you."

The tears ran down her cheeks and pooled at the top of the tape.

"Did you really think I was going to just let you walk away with *my* money?" he asked her as he rose from behind the desk.

She shook her head frantically. It was her money. Jeff was crazy. If he had just behaved like family and accepted her she probably would've shared her inheritance with him.

"That's right, no," he said.

He was close enough for him to feel his hot breath on her face. She strained backward as far as she could to escape him.

"I don't know who you are and I don't care. Somehow you and that lawyer convinced my holier-than-thou uncle that you were his love child. Maybe you're in on it together."

She shook her head again. He laughed and pinched her chin sharply, forcing her to look him in the eye as he spoke, "I don't care if you are or not. I don't care about you at all. That money was rightfully mine. I am a Donovan. Do you think it was my fault that my father was a despotic old fool who bankrupted us while paying for his whores and gambling?"

He released her and she shook her head ever so slightly before letting it drop.

Megan had read somewhere that wounded animals were the most dangerous and Jeff Donovan seemed like a wounded animal. She could smell the desperation in his sweat as she was sure he could smell the fear in hers.

"I'm sure you're wondering why I have you here. Why this is necessary. Why Ivy League educated man such as myself would stoop to such tactics. The truth is I need something from you, Miss Black. I need you to sign over the accounts to me and before the night is through you'll do just as I say. You wouldn't know what to do with that kind of money anyway. I could tell at first glance you were nothing but trash," he said in disgust.

"I'm sure you're also wondering why the haste. My father left some rather large debts with some unsavory people who would do me harm if given the chance. I don't intend to allow that to happen. I don't intend for some piece of trash to be the reason that that happens."

He ripped the tape from her mouth and Megan felt like her lips came off with it. She took a couple of gulps of air gratefully but she remained silent which took all of her willpower. She wanted to scream that he could go fuck himself but she knew that it would only make her predicament worse.

"That's better isn't it?" he asked cordially.

Megan nodded yes.

"Good. Now, I have the account all set up for you to transfer the funds to. I also have the documents for you to sign when we're through," he told her.

He sounded eager. Too eager. It couldn't be as easy as her giving him the money. Wasn't he afraid that she'd call the authorities?

A new level of panic gripped Megan and she was afraid she may faint. She didn't want to ask but knew she had to.

"What will you do with me after?"

He looked at her as if she were simple and spoke the words she dreaded, "Why, I'll kill you of course."

Megan slumped in her chair. She needed to keep a level head and figure a way out of her current predicament but finding her calm while in imminent danger was near impossible. She tried to wiggle her legs and arms to test her bonds but they didn't give at all.

"Don't bother to struggle. You're only going to make this worse. I promise you that it will be over quickly once our business is done," he tried to reassure her but was only heightening her sense of terror.

Think Megan. Think!

She knew that signing those papers would be signing her own death warrant. She had to figure out a way out of this. Her brain started working on overdrive. He'd have to release at least one of her hands for her signature and that would be her time to act and she'd have to do so quickly.

Megan closed her eyes and brought the room to mind like looking at a photograph. She could see the open door and the overstuffed bookshelves on one wall near the fireplace. There was nothing on the built in shelves that would be any use but there were a brass shovel and a poker hanging from the rack of firewood. The poker would make a good weapon but the chances of her reaching it were slim. She made a mental note of it just in case and moved clockwise to the next wall.

In front of the large windows were two Louis the IV chairs like the one she was bound to with a carved pedestal table between them. On the table lay a book and nothing else of use. She could probably use the furniture if she had to but she dismissed that area. The chairs were too heavy.

The opposite wall was in her mind's eye next. The

wallpapered wall held a large, gilt-framed canvas of a pastoral landscape in between two wall sconces. Below it was a console, its draws flung open with papers falling out onto the Persian rug. On its marble inlaid top was a heap of even more papers including the letters to her mother that she had set aside and tied together with a red ribbon she had found with them. Megan recalled how the console looked before it was ransacked and remembered that on the left of the bundle of letters was a sharp knife-like letter opener with a rosewood handle near the second drawer. *Bingo!* She may have to dig to find it if it was disturbed from its original placement but knowing it was there bolstered her.

Finally, she moved on to the part of the room where Jeff was. He sat in the overlarge wingchair with a laptop open in front of him. The heavy striped curtains on the windows were drawn and most of the draws of the desk were opened, the rest were upended on the floor surrounding it. Papers were scattered everywhere and her father's journals had been carelessly knocked over. The black rotary phone was on the right side and she could see that the wires were still intact. Her coffee mug from that morning was also amongst the debris of paper on the desktop and so was a small tiffany lamp. Any of those would most likely be within her reach.

She formulated a plan. If she could muster enough force she'd hit him with either the heavy mug or the lamp or even the laptop and hopefully knock him out long enough to grab the letter opener. She'd have to dial the police quickly. She closed her eyes again and focused on the small pad that was usually kept by the phone with its list of numbers. She mentally scanned the list until she knew them all. Two-one-two. The emergency number she'd need to call. The only problem left to solve was how to free her legs.

Megan was already feeling the painful pins and needles stabbing into her from the poor circulation. She could feel her stockings slipping down, ripped away from her garters from the struggle on the lawn. She started wiggling her backside in the chair.

"I told you not to bother. I'm just setting up the account now. You won't have long to wait," he said without looking up.

"My butt is just falling asleep," she lied.

He shook his head in disgust and muttered, "Trash," and resumed his typing.

A single piece of silk hosiery started contracting down her thigh until it rolled against the tape at her ankle. She started flexing and unflexing carefully but nothing happened. She realized that it wasn't going to work. She tried a new approach. She strained sideways until the tape felt like it would give. She moaned in frustration. Megan sent up a silent prayer that she would be able to pull this off and another that if needed, she'd have the strength and courage to use the letter opener if she could get to it.

Jeff rose from behind the desk and stepped over the wreckage.

"Seems like your times up," he said and she quaked in fear. She was going to have to improvise.

He pulled a pocketknife from his trousers and she flinched but he was only leaning in to cut her wrists free. It was go time. She grabbed him with both hands and bit down hard on his shoulder.

"You little Bitch!" he screeched and backhanded her across the face.

Her eyes watered and she could taste copper in her mouth from where her teeth cut the inside of her cheek.

"You can't hope to get away with this Jeff! People know where I am! My family knows where I am! You're going to get caught. You know what happens to soft little rich boys in prison Jeff?" she taunted, desperately trying to stall long enough to see reason and for her to get her legs free.

She clawed frantically at the tape.

He struck her again, "Enough! You're going to give me that password!"

"If I don't? You can't kill me 'til you get it and I'm tougher than you think. You won't be able to beat it out of me Jeff."

This wasn't false bravado. Adrenaline was coursing through her veins. It was fight or flight and she knew that the latter wasn't an option until she could get free.

"Oh, I think you'll give it to me," he said and pulled out a nickel plated pistol that had been concealed somewhere under his blazer and pressed it to her temple.

CHAPTER 15

Gabe was standing outside his bedroom window, gazing at the closed curtains of Megan's apartment feeling sorry for himself. It had been almost a week since she had bolted from his home, shutting the door on any chance he had of making things right. He had tried to call that next day her but she kept sending him to voicemail. He had been tempted to show up at her door but realized he probably wouldn't be welcome there.

He wondered for the hundredth time what she was doing and if she was hurting as bad as he was. He tried to go about his life but everything seemed dull without her. His senses were beginning to fade but this time he wasn't sure if it was the curse taking effect on him once more or if he was simply depressed. All he knew was that Megan had brought light into his life and with her gone, he was alone with his own darkness.

Gabe went in to fix himself a nightcap in hopes that it would put him to sleep. So far it hadn't worked but he was desperate to see her face even if it was in his dreams.

He tipped the bottle over the glass, filling it to the

brim with the golden spirit and as he was stoppering the bottle he felt a shiver run up his spine. It was as if someone had walked across his grave. He had tried to shake the feeling and go back to drinking but the sense that something wasn't right nagged at him. He left near full glass where it was and climbed into bed, attempting to close his eyes to the uneasiness.

"Megan!" Gabe called up as he sat bolt upright against the pillows.

He dreamed she was in peril and was calling out to him. He threw back the comforter and got dressed quickly, intending to go over to her place and check on her, welcome or not.

On his way, he dialed her number repeatedly but the voicemail picked up before it even rang as if it were turned off. The sickening feeling of dread was enough to make him double over. He straightened himself out and took a few deep breaths and began running.

The touch of cold steel against her skin stilled her immediately. The knowledge that there would be no escape, no plan to try, quelled her. She knew that she would die alone, far from home, far from anyone who loved her. Memories and fragments of her life flitted before her. Her first trip to the zoo, Uncle Ham's big arms, Gayle laughing, her mother singing, jumping in a pile of leaves.

Though she wasn't religious, she began praying fervently in her mind, *"Please God, if you can hear me I know I haven't been the best person but I don't want to die. If I have to though please take care of my Ma. I don't know if she could handle it. Please take care of Ham and Gayle too."*

She thought of Gabe and her heart ached. She regretted that she'd never get to see him again and tell him she loved him. *Oh, Gabe! I don't care what you've done. I forgive you and I'm sorry. I was so angry I lost sight of what you meant to me. Maybe I was just scared and now I'm afraid you'll never know how much I loved you. If you were here I'd never let you go again. Please, Da protect me. If you really have an angel watching over me please send him now."*

"Type in the passcode," Jeff's voice broke through her supplication and her fingers trembled. "Hurry up!" he demanded and pushed the gun up against her brutally.

Megan began typing in the digits in sequence, one at

a time. She got to the last one and she hesitated, knowing that a bullet would probably go through her brain before her hand ever left the keyboard. She still couldn't reconcile that her life would end violently and without a fight.

"What the…" she heard Jeff say and went deaf with the discharge of a gunshot.

Megan thought perhaps she was dead but when she opened her eyes she realized that she was still in the room and barrel was no longer pressed against her head. She turned just in time to see Gabe holding Jeff in the air, his Burberry wingtips dangling in the air.

She was too stunned to speak. Jeff dropped the gun and it thumped to the floor as Gabe lowered him into his arms and put his mouth to his. Megan wondered if maybe she had really been killed or out cold and was dreaming the scene before her but the pain in her face and the taste of blood was enough to assure her she wasn't.

"Holy fucking shit," she said in a whisper as she watched a blue-like light being sucked from Jeff's mouth into Gabe's. Gabe's whole body seemed to glow in response. Almost too bright and too beautiful for him to look at. In a flash, it was over. When the light was gone her deranged cousin went slack. Gabe let the body fall to the floor and then he reached out to her. She shrunk back at his outstretched hand.

"What the fuck was that? What are you?" she asked him stunned and scared by what she saw.

Gabe thought long and hard for a minute. He was in shock himself at having been somehow transported to her side right as the man on the floor was just about to pull the trigger on the gun against her head.

He sat down hard on an empty chair. His arm rubbed against the duct tape on the carved arm and he looked down at it, absently plucking a silvery piece up to examine before letting it drop to the floor. Blood was dripping down his leg but he didn't seem to notice. Instead, he took in the disarray of the study and the bruised and frightened look on her face. He wasn't sure what happened there, wherever there even was. He decided to go with the truth and hoped she could handle it.

"What was that, you ask. That was me saving your life, Megan," he said, suddenly sounding exhausted.

She still had a bewildered look on her swollen face but she answered, "Thank you for that but I'm still not sure how you came to be in Ireland, in this room, at just the right time. And what did you do to him?" she pointed to the motionless body on the floor though she kept her green eyes averted, "What was that light? Did you just kill him? How?"

"There's a lot I need to explain to you, Megan. I know that. I also have a couple of questions myself that I hope we can find the answers to together but first I think we need to call Mr. McCredie and then we need to call the police," he told her.

Megan's head was spinning. She somehow wasn't surprised to hear that he was acquainted with her father's lawyer. Since reading the journals she had suspected that Gabe was the man Mr. McCredie had hired to watch her. It made a strange kind of sense although not much else did.

"Why McCredie first?" she asked him.

"Because the police are going to wonder how I came to be in this country with no identification whatsoever. I'm also pretty sure that explaining what happened to him," he nodded his head in the direction of Jeff's body, "Is also going to be hard."

She may have been distrustful and even a little afraid of him, but Gabe did save her life and she didn't want to see him rot in a foreign prison for it. He may have taken a life in exchange for hers but she felt no remorse for the loss of the man who was trying to take all from her and discard her like the trash he insisted she was.

"Ok. Let's see what Uncle Peter has to say," and she giggled out of nerves.

The EMT's had put a blanket around Megan's shoulders and were examining her as she sat in an ambulance outside of the vicarage. Gabe was sitting on a gurney, Mr. McCredie standing while giving a statement to two uniformed men with notepads and pens as a stretcher with a white sheet draped over it was being wheeled out. Every so often they would shoot glances in her direction.

"You take it easy now Miss. Yer gonna want ta go real slow like while eatin' or talkin' fer a day or two," the young man examining her said at last.

After some poking and prodding and having a flashlight shined in her eyes, she was finally cleared to go. She had some minor contusions and abrasions and her cheek had a nasty cut on the inside that wouldn't require stitches but she didn't have any broken bones or a concussion.

"You'll have ta go to the hospital in case o' shock.

We'll be leaving in a moment. Tis a miracle ya know. You're lucky ta be alive."

He closed his bag and left her standing alone as he strode back toward where the other ambulances were parked. She wondered if it was indeed a miracle and if her father was somehow watching over her. She found the thought comforting.

"Yes, it is a miracle," she said to no one.

CHAPTER 16

They were released from the hospital hours later. She was fully cleared and was told by Mr. McCredie that the bullet had only grazed Gabe's leg and that he only needed stitches just as she saw them wheel him out to the front entrance where they were standing by the lawyer's car. Megan had a sudden jolt of guilt and concern as she watched Gabe pull himself up from the chair and limp over to where they stood. Mr. McCredie said that they obviously couldn't go back to the vicarage until it was cleared by the local law enforcement, not that she wanted to, so the lawyer had made other arrangements.

McCredie had booked them luxury accommodations inside the beautiful old castle where Megan had dined that very evening. She couldn't believe it was only hours before that she had been there eating her way through a mountain of vegetables and succulent lamb in the opulent dining room below. It seemed like months had passed since then. It all felt surreal.

Gabe insisted they share a room when the Lawyer was calling ahead to book their stay. Peter raised a brow at Gabe's insistence and clapped a hand over the receiver waiting for some sort of reply. Gabe complied.

"I don't want her to be alone. She'll be fine with it. Just book it."

McCredie seemed to think that was a good enough reason as any and said into the phone, "Looks like a change o' plans. I'll be just needin' the one room then but I may call back ta take the other. Brilliant! Thanks," he said and hung up.

When Peter told Megan about the rooms she looked to Gabe for an explanation. He used the excuses he gave the squat older man and then he promised he'd explain the 'other things' she wanted to know about, as a way to get inside the door with her approval. She told the lawyer it was okay and they set off for the castle.

The car ride had been awkwardly silent with her alone in the back because Gabe needed room for his leg and she used the quiet to recall the events that transpired that night. If Megan had believed that traveling with him was awkward, entering the decadently romantic suite with him was even more so.

Neither looked at the bed even though Megan's sore body ached to lie down in its softness and find oblivion.

Instead, they each took one of the slipper chairs by a dining table and stared in their laps for a long time, Gabe with his injured leg propped on an ottoman.

There was a knock at the door and Megan jumped. Gabe rose to limp over to the door and after peering through the peephole, opened it wide. A bellboy in a black vest and white shirt wheeled in a cart. He was either extremely polite or very well trained because his face did not change in the slightest if he had noticed her bruised face or dirty clothes as he took a silver tea service and tray of pastries off the cart and placed them on the table before her.

He asked her if she'd be needing anything else and she was tempted to ask for a bourbon but instead shook her head no. She knew better than anyone that alcohol was not going to solve her problems. Gabe handed the boy a tip after digging through his faded jeans and signed the slip of paper he was handed. He waited for the boy to nod his thanks and closed the door behind him, leaving them alone once more.

Gabe poured out two cups of steaming hot cocoa into the delicate china cups and set one by her hand and resumed his seat. He waited for her to take a sip and curl up comfortably before starting.

"A long time ago I saw a woman walking in the fields carrying a large basket full of carrots. She wasn't very beautiful but there was something about her that called to me. I began watching her day after day as she went about her life. She always seemed so full of joy though I had witnessed how little to be joyful she had. Sometimes she would talk out loud as if she could see me there while hanging her laundry or fetching water at the brook. She had a very soft voice like the whisper of a butterfly wing. I wanted very much to talk back to her. To let her know I was there but it was against the rules.

I spent the next year or so as her shadow. I would watch a lock of golden hair fall across her smooth cheek as she worked and wish to put it back in its place or see her straining to lift a heavy burden and wish to carry it for her but all was forbidden to me. I'd watch her sleep and wish to kiss her brow. I was enamored of her.

One day, not long after finding her, a holy war broke out in that part of Éire. The Cogadh an Dá Rí had been going on for some time but the battle of Aughrim was raging on, practically at their door. My lovely Mary, as I had begun to think of her as mine, was in grave danger.

When the fighting was done they were the only

villagers for miles and miles around that survived the bloodshed that took more than seven thousand Irish lives. By the grace of some miracle, they were spared only to face starvation as the fields had been stripped bare by the mass of soldiers that had marched through. I wanted very much to help them so I would go out to the fields and bring back whatever I could. Sometimes I would find some loaves of bread or a basket of fish in the army camps that were close by and take it. I would put it all in her basket for her to find in the morning. Mary was very devout and every morning she woke to see my gifts she'd drop to her knees in supplication and prayer. Sometimes she would turn directly to me and say thank you as if she knew I was there and what I had done.

It wasn't too long after the fighting ended that Mary and her family were to be forced off their land despite my efforts to keep them safely there. They loaded what belongings in their wagon that they could fit and set off across the country on foot, pulling it behind them as they had no livestock left and the horse had been taken long ago, most likely from a soldier or someone fleeing the battle. I followed behind them on their arduous journey just far enough away to not be intrusive but close enough to watch and help as needed.

Somewhere on the road after more than a fortnight of walking, Mary became ill. I continued to fill her basket with food but she was wasting away. Her already willowy frame was so thin as you could see the bones of her skull just beneath her face. The light was slowly fading from her and the family had to stop frequently for her to rest. She trailed far behind the wagon and would talk to me more and more. She told me she was dying and had been for some time. I didn't want it to be so. I didn't understand what was happening to her. She was fading before my eyes. My smiling Mary didn't smile much anymore. Her bright eyes were dulled and she was racked by pain most of the time and there was nothing I could do to ease it. It all seemed so unfair. Not only had this beautiful, innocent creature been forced to live a life of turmoil and loss, but then all the prayers she gave out were answered with this wasting disease.

Maybe the most ironic part was as she grew worse the connection between us grew deeper. Not only would she talk to me but she could both see and touch me. She would hold my hand when no one was looking and I was able to lift her up and carry her when needed. She spoke of what heaven would be like and the things she loved most of all. The tastes and sounds and sights. She described them so well that I felt like I was experiencing her memories with her. It was wonderful.

One night as Mary lay in a meadow to sleep, I lay beside her. She turned to face me and looked right into mine with her eyes the color of a clear sky and still beautiful despite being sunken and bruised in her hollow face. She called me her angel and told me again how she was dying. I could tell the pain was getting to be unbearable and she wouldn't be much longer for this world. It was incredibly selfish of me but I wanted to kiss her just the once before she passed. I hoped that maybe I could somehow take her suffering upon myself but when I pressed my lips to hers she grew peaceful. I had felt her life-force enter my body and wept with all of her beautiful memories and thoughts that were what made her herself. When I opened my eyes Mary was no more. She lay still on the grass. I supposed I had succeeded in removing her pain because my kiss was the kiss of death. It had taken her away forever."

A single tear rolled down the groove in between the place where his nose met his pale cheek. Megan fought back the urge to wipe it away along and smooth back his furrowed brow. Instead, she offered what she could.

"I'm sorry Gabe but it wasn't your fault. She was

dying anyway."

"I know that but that was only the first of my sins. I also thought what happened following that time was some sort of retribution for my actions with Mary," he said, sounding anguished.

Megan padded across the room and brought over a box of tissues. She used one to blot her own eyes and handed one to Gabe.

"Thanks," he said as he took the soft paper.

Megan sat back down and refilled both their mugs just to warm them and resumed her seat.

"What other sins?" she asked him curiously, trying to hide her trepidation over his answer behind her cup.

Gabe shifted in his chair and moved his leg a little before turning his gray gaze once more to her and resuming his confession.

"I could not return home after Mary's death. It was if I had amnesia or something. I couldn't remember where I had come from or who I even was, save for the name Mary called me. The only memories I had were Mary's or of Mary and her family and the area around their farm. Whatever had been before was lost to me in the moment I laid Mary down on that field. I had nowhere else to go so I stayed in Ireland long enough to witness firsthand the wars and the blight, the famine, and the bloody civil wars. It was during those times I had also embraced the fact that I was a monster.

I needed no sustenance as other people did. I could eat food and take drink but none of it had any flavor and it couldn't sate me. I felt a terrible need to feed upon the life-force of others and I had done so often. I would choose the wicked. The rapists and the murderers and the like and would take my fill there. I had always been good at watching others without them seeing me and it was easy to spot those who did evil. I don't want you to think I was good because I wasn't. I was still a killer though I never wanted to take the life of an innocent again although through some strange mercy I would sometimes go to those dying or wishing to die. I wasn't good or just at all. I killed because I enjoyed it. Feeding was the only time I felt anything. It was if I was taking in the life of the person, their joys, their fears, their pain, their love all in a second and making their very essence, their lives, my own.

After a while, I had learned to control the craving and later the killing. I learned that I didn't have to take it all though sometimes I still did."

He stopped talking for a moment and took a sip of

the cold chocolate, marveling at the taste, and looked up at her to gage her reaction to the admission of being a vampire. Her green eyes gave away nothing.

Gabe told her how he had been forced, after those first few years of confusion, to take on the name of Mary's family and try to fit in amongst the people.

He had eventually joined the military where his ability to kill silently and to remain hidden and gather information made him an excellent spy although he said every so often he'd have to fake his own death and reenlist almost a lifetime later. When he was in those between times he would take on odd jobs like farming or fishing or even blacksmithing.

He told her about being away fighting in World War One and coming home to civil unrest and the war of independence that followed and his service there. His exploits continued into WWII. Ireland had declared itself neutral but lent out its spies to the America's. Later he had joined the IRA as an intelligence agent.

"So how did you end up immigrating to America?" she asked him.

"Well, sometime in the fifties I had gotten some fake papers drawn up by an IRA member and I had them doctored. It was much easier then to travel to a foreign country," he told her.

"But why Boston? Why then?" she clarified her question.

He put down his cup and tasted one of the delicate petite fours, appreciating the rich chocolate and moist cake with cream inside.

"Since Mary, I had made a sort of promise to myself. She still had a family she had left behind, a mother and father and younger brother and I had made sure they had made it safely to their destination. I owed them that much. I made sure to bring them food or money as I earned it or found it. All anonymously.

As the years passed I continued to look in on her family. Her brother had many children and when they grew I'd look out for their children and so forth and so on. After so many years the family got smaller or more diluted and eventually the youngest son left for the states. I went too and watched him there and his family when he had one. Not all the time but I would check in once every year or two to see how they were," he explained.

His reply clarified so much yet so little. Megan found herself torn between seeing how it made total sense and being completely at sea because of the timeline and the fact that he was talking about immortality. She decided to ask about something more tangible to her.

"Where do I come in?" she asked.

"I'm getting to it," he assured her, "Here, you need to lie down Megan. Why don't you lay down and I'll finish my story and I'll answer your questions as well as I can."

"Fine," she consented and stiffly rose from the chair and lumbered over to lay on the lacy coverlet.

He sat lay down beside her at a safe distance and propped his head up on his hand.

When he was sure she was comfortable he continued, "McCredie hired me to check up on a young woman though he didn't tell me why or for who so I did. It was a decent paycheck. I do some work as a private dick ever now and then since I'm so good at watching people."

"And I was the woman you were supposed to shadow?" she cut in feeling miffed.

"Yes, and at some point, the job had ended but I would still check in on you from time to time although it wasn't the same as checking on the Donovan's'."

"Wait!" she held up a hand, "As in Donovan? As in Jeff Donovan the man you...The man that attacked me?"

she corrected herself.

He looked stricken, "That man was a Donovan! I killed the last of Mary's line?"

Megan was reeling too much to answer him right away but she finally returned with her own question, "So would that make Jonathan Lucas Donovan Mary's great-great-great-great grandnephew too or whatever?"

Gabe looked just as confounded as her.

"I'm lost at your line of questioning. I admit I saw the clipping in your apartment but I didn't know how you knew the man or why this matters other than that I truly am damned. Yes, I knew him all his life but I'm not sure he knew me. Or maybe he did. He reminded me of Mary that way. Always looking right at me even when I was hidden. He had gone off to Ireland and I hadn't the courage to return there after being gone so long. I didn't want to be reminded of my sins. It seems I can't escape them, maybe never could because here I am once more and this time I've killed the last Donovan."

"No, you haven't," she told him.

"Megan, I know you may wish to make me feel better but I know what I've done," he said miserably.

"No. You haven't killed the last Donovan, Gabe, because I am the last Donovan," she said quickly.

"Your name is Black," he said stupidly.

She laughed at his failure to catch on, "Yes, my name is Black, same as my mother's because I'm a bastard, Gabe. My father, on the other hand, was the late great Reverend Johnathan Lucas Donovan. They conceived me here in Ireland and then lost touch with one another. The only reason he knew about me or I about him was because of you. McCredie hired you to look into me because he knew that I was Luke's."

Saying it out loud made her wonder how much of life was just twists of fate and coincidence or if it was all some sort of destiny. The thought made the hair on the back of her neck stand on end and she wondered if Gabe was having the same eerie feeling.

"That's unbelievable, Megan!" he said elated and surprised.

"No shit!" she said summarily.

They fell asleep separately but had somehow drifted together in the night so that their bodies touched from forehead to toe. If either of them had woke to discover their position they didn't bother to do anything about it.

When they did finally awaken at the same time, they immediately shied away from each other awkwardly.

"Shall I call up for breakfast?" Gabe asked her.

The night before was the first time that Megan had ever had room service and she found the novelty delightful. She found a menu in the bedside table and began perusing it while naming their choices out loud.

A different bellboy than the last brought them their breakfast. He seemed just as well trained as the other because he didn't take notice of her appearance or the absurd amount of food they ordered either. He poured out their coffee and politely left the room, entreating them to enjoy.

Despite the Doctor's recommendation that she only eat soft foods, Megan tore into one of the Belgian waffles topped with fresh whipped cream and strawberries and squealed.

"Does your mouth hurt?" he asked, concerned.

"Who cares? These are fabulous!" she said and took another bite.

Gabe smiled at her, thinking her adorable but when he tasted them himself he wanted to squeal too.

He had told Megan about how he had only recently regained his sense of taste as they were choosing from the menu and she had insisted that they order one of every kind of breakfast food. If he hadn't already loved her he would have just for that. It amazed him how thoughtful she was.

"Try the blueberry crepes," she insisted with a full mouth and pointed to them with her fork. She was rewarded with a moan of ecstasy he let out when he bit into the rolled delicacy made her smile.

They devoured most of everything except for the black and white pudding, which both agreed looked disgusting. They sat in their chairs sipping coffee though they both complained they couldn't really fit it in their bellies.

"So tell me," she began as she took a sip, "What kind of things did you watch me do?"

She hoped his answer wouldn't embarrass her too much.

"Let me see. I was at your graduation and the day you moved in to your apartment with Gayle. I was at your twenty-fifth birthday where your friends hired a stripper."

She turned red to the roots of her hair which was probably the only place it would be noticed because of the bruising.

"Mostly I watched you paint," he admitted.

"I paint naked," she said, feeling flush.

He flashed a full-toothed grin.

"Yes, you do. Most of the time. I have to admit, the nights you put on that ugly flannel thing I was sorely disappointed."

"Good. I packed it with me. Is that why you kept on watching me? Because you're a pervert?" she asked with a mixture of teasing and seriousness.

"It was definitely a perk. You are very beautiful Megan," he said and she felt a warm tingle between her thighs, "But mostly I just liked watching you. You have a way about you. You're kind to others especially those in need. You have a quirky way of talking to yourself when you're mulling something over. You eat like a draft horse. You seem to appreciate everything and take nothing for granted. You're cautious and shy around others but when you're in your element you're like some wild thing who commands her surroundings with a confidence of a queen. Plus you look good naked. Did I mention that?"

The list of her best qualities that she hadn't even realized touched her heart until the end which had her plucking the pillow out from under his propped leg and throwing it at his laughing face.

"Ouch! Careful now. You don't want to attack a

wounded man?" he asked.

"Sorry," She apologized.

She had forgotten about his stitches.

"It's okay. I'm surprised it hasn't healed yet and I'm not accustomed to feeling pain," he explained.

"You mean because of the whole immortal thing?" she asked him.

She had almost forgotten about that part. She wanted to understand it better. To understand him better.

He pulled down the pant leg of his pajama bottoms and pulled off the bandage. There was an ugly mark with neat stitching crossing it.

"Actually I guess I can't call myself that anymore I don't think."

What do you mean?" she asked him, concerned.

He reapplied the gauze pad and pulled his pants back up before looking at her, "I mean I've never been able to be hurt before. Not really. If I'd been wounded it had only ever been for but a moment before I'd heal."

Megan thought really hard. *Had he really become mortal? Why?* She repeated her thoughts out loud. "Why now? What does it mean?"

"I'm not sure," he admitteded.

CHAPTER 17

They had eaten lunch in a private booth in the dining room. Megan had asked Gabe all sorts of questions as they ate but they hadn't really come to any conclusions about his origins by the time they retired back to the suite for a nap.

Someone knocked on the door and woke Megan and she got up and stood on tiptoe to peer through the peephole. A man in plain clothes with a badge hanging from his neck was standing there. She unlocked the door but left the chain in place.

"Miss Megan Black?" he asked.

She looked over to the bed where Gabe still slept soundly and turned back to the man standing in the hall.

"Yes. Can I help you?" she asked quietly.

He held up the badge.

"I'm with the Clifden police. I hope I'm not disturbin' you but I have a few questions I need to ask you."

She looked back to the bed again.

"Actually now is not the best time," she told him.

"Sorry. I suppose I can go over to Mr. O'Niel's room and speak to him and then come back up here when I'm done if it's alright," he proposed.

Megan wondered who Mr. O'Neil was but then remembered that was the last name that Gabe had adopted for the sake of the police. She had to decide what to do. She knew the officer would be back because there was no one in Gabe's room. Actually, he had cancelled the room altogether since he was staying with her.

"Hold on a minute," she grumped at him as she closed the door.

She went to the bed and took Gabe's muscled shoulder in her hand and shook him gently.

"Gabe. Wake up. The police want to talk to us."

"What?" he asked groggily.

"There's a police officer here who wants to ask us some questions," she whispered.

She was trying hard not to be nervous. She was

hoping that at least with them both being asked questions they could corroborate each other's stories. She wasn't a very experienced liar and didn't want to say something that would put Gabe behind bars.

"Should we call Mr. McCredie?" she asked him.

"No. It will only look suspicious. We'll be fine if we do this together," he said and got up and pulled the t-shirt he had discarded back on and moved to the table where he sat down and put his foot up.

He nodded to her and she went back to the door. She undid the final lock and opened it.

"Sorry, we were just taking a nap," she excused rudeness.

He took a couple of steps in behind her, "You have a guest?" he asked.

"Yes, actually. It's Mr. O'Neil," she answered as she strode the rest of the way in.

If the man raised a brow but didn't say anything about it besides, "Lovely. Now I can speak to the both of you."

Gabe took his foot off the ottoman and raised himself up enough to shake the other man's hand and offer him a seat. Megan had already sat down opposite Gabe so the officer had to sit in the middle.

"I'm sorry to barge in on you two. I'm sure you need your rest after all you've been through so I promise I'll try and keep it brief," he was polite.

"Thank you, officer…?" Megan trailed off in askance.

"Black. Detective Michael Black at your service." He introduced himself.

"What a coincidence," Megan said with a smile.

The detective looked suddenly uncomfortable. "Actually it's not so much a coincidence, I'm afraid. I had to look into your background. Your mother is my sister."

"Holy fucking shit!" Megan said.

Detective Black looked at her in shock at her language but then he smiled.

"Yes. But I suppose that's a conversation for another time," he dismissed her and the subject, "The reason I'm here is that I have some questions to ask before I send this out to INTERPOL. I'll also be recording this. First I'll start with you Miss Black if that's alright?"

It was more of a direction than a question so she nodded assent as he set the recorder on the table and pressed a button.

"Your lawyer said that the first time you had ever

met Jeff Donovan was in his office," he stated.

Megan wasn't sure if she was supposed to say anything since it wasn't phrased as a question so she nodded.

"I'll need you to say yes if the statement is true and no if it's false. If I ask a question I'll need you to answer truthfully to the best of your knowledge. Do you understand?" he clarified the process for her.

"Yes, and yes, I met Jeff Donovan in Mr. McCredie's office for the first time during the reading of my father's will," she answered.

"Did Jeff Donovan seem upset or irate at that reading?" he asked.

"Yes. He seemed really upset that he didn't inherit anything and had threatened me although at the time I thought he was just blowing off steam," she answered.

"Were you aware of Jeff Donovan's financial situation?" he asked.

She answered, "No. I had only just met him and he didn't mention it then."

He smiled with the assurance that she was doing a good job, "Did you see Jeff Donovan again at any time between the time he left Mr. McCredie's office and the time you found him in the vicarage?"

"No," she said.

"Can you tell me as best you can recall, what happened last night leading up to you finding Jeff Donovan in the vicarage?"

She motioned for Gabe to pour her some water from the pitcher on the table before she began speaking, "I came here, to the castle for dinner in my father's car. I had gotten permission from my father's attorney to drive it," she assured him. He nodded and she continued, "I had the lamb and some cake and I drove back."

"Did you have anything to drink?" Detective Black interjected with his question.

"Yes. I had about two sips of champagne," she admitted.

He made a note on his pad.

"You can continue Miss Black. I'm only marking it down in case it explains any lapses in memory or lessoned your ability to defend yourself. Don't worry."

"Okay. So I drove back and when I was coming on to the house I noticed the lights were on. I remember thinking it was funny. When I went to the door it was unlocked so I went inside. I heard a noise in my father's office so I went to check it out. I know it was stupid. I should have called the police right away but I didn't know if I had been the one to leave the lights on and the door open and if some person who worked for the church was inside. I saw Jeff in the room digging through my father's things. I tried to go back outside but he jumped me. We fought and I hit him and made it outside but he attacked me again and broke my phone. Then he tied me up and demanded I give him the account information for my inheritance. Then he pulled a gun and put it to my head. Gabe stopped him just in time," she felt herself shaking as she told her harrowing tale.

"That'll do Megan. It's over now. You can rest easy." He said and patted her hand. Gabe had grabbed her other one from across the table and squeezed it comfortingly. The detective turned to Gabe.

"So you were there in the nick of time it seems. How did you come to be there at all?" he asked him.

"Megan had given me a ticket and invited me to Ireland with her but I was being an ass and stayed behind. I realized that I was being a fool to let my girlfriend go alone under such sad circumstances even if she had broken up with me," Megan glared at him from across the table but he pretended not to notice, "so I got on a plane and went to find her. I remembered her mentioning McCredie so I called him up from the airport and asked if he'd seen her. He told me where she was. When I arrived the door was wide open so I went in. There was a man yelling so I followed his voice. The man had a gun to Megan's head so I went after him. Picked him up in the air with both hands. The gun went off. I think I was in shock. It all happened so quickly. I remember dropping him and running to Megan. I thought maybe he just passed out or that he had shot himself in the struggle. He was just lying there. Megan didn't know the number for the police so she called McCredie and he phoned them for her. I didn't even know that I was the one shot until someone told me I was bleeding," he told the lie he went over with Peter easily. Megan wasn't sure why the lawyer was covering for him but she was grateful.

"I guess that's all I need then."

The detective tucked his recorder in his pocket and rose.

"One more thing," he said and Megan's heart gave a lurch. She was sure they were caught. "Can you ask Josephine to call me?" he asked and handed her a card. "And I'd love to have some time with you too before you leave for the states," he said and left the room, closing the door behind him leaving Megan to gawp.

That night Megan and Gabe snuggled together in bed.

"You think you'll ever love me again?" Gabe asked her in the darkness.

"How do you know I loved you?" she asked him.

He ran a hand up her arm.

"Because I heard you say it. It was like a dream but I knew it was real. You were telling me how sorry you were and that you loved me.

The hair on the back of her head stood on end.

"I was praying. I thought I was going to die. I asked for an angel and you came and saved me.

"I'm no angel," he told her.

She slid her hand up his back, "Yes you are. Even my father said you were. In his journal, he said you were an angel and you didn't know it. That he had prayed for an angel to watch over me and there you were."

"Did he really say that?" he asked.

"Yes. He said that being so near death made it easy to see angels and that he knew you for what you really were. That you weren't a monster, you only thought so."

"Hmm."

He seemed to be taking it in.

"And you heard me all the way from America and

came to me by magic to save me after I prayed for you," she said.

"I suppose I did. That wasn't the first time you had called me to you like that," he told her.

"What do you mean?" she asked him, the hand on his back stilled.

"I mean you would call me away to make love to you. It was like a dream but I wasn't sleeping," he said and she felt him stiffen against her thigh.

"That was real?" she asked, completely stunned and embarrassed.

"You mean when you and I danced in your apartment? Or when I carried you to the bed and worshiped you with my tongue and hands until you cried out? Or when I slid inside you and we found heaven together? Then? Yes. That was very real," he said huskily.

Megan's body ached for him to kiss her all over like that again.

"That was my first time you know," she told him.

"Mine too," he said and captured her mouth with his.

They made love slowly, exploring each other's body anew. He rained kisses down every part of her body sending shimmers of delight across her supple skin before parting her legs and dipping his head between them to lave at her most sensitive of places. She exploded in millions of shooting stars but he kept on going.

"My turn," she said at last and he rolled over onto his back.

She kissed him all over as he did for her, pressing her lips to his taut nipples and down his belly and his thighs. He moaned, urging her to bolden her exploration. She took him fully in her mouth. She savored the sensation, like velvet over steal as she bobbed her head up and down, imitating the motion of making love. He tangled his hands in her hair as he groaned in pleasure. She kept going.

"Megan stop," he said although every nerve in his body screamed for her to keep going.

She looked up and met his eyes while still suckling him and he was almost undone. He pulled her away and flipped her underneath him on the bed.

"I love you, Megan," he told her and plunged inside of her.

He kept the pace slow. Each stroke was agonizingly expert, bringing her to new heights of pleasure as he filled her one slow inch at a time, pushing deeper and deeper inside of her.

"I love you too, Gabriel," she panted, "But now it's my turn," she told him and rolled him off her.

She braced her hands on his muscled pecs as she speared herself on him over and over. He reached up to cup her breasts in his hands, rubbing his thumbs across her nipples in a circular motion. She sat up straight, changing the pressure so that his thick head glided against that spot inside of her that felt like magic. She moaned and tipped her head back while undulating her hips. He released her breasts and grabbed hold of her cheeks, lifting her slowly as she rose and grinding her into him when she landed. Their moans increased and he tilted his head up to capture a nipple in his mouth to suckle as he lifted off the bed to meet her as she crashed into him with increasing speed. He rolled her again, pinning her hips to the bed with his own. She squealed and he kissed her deeply, his tongue sliding in and out of her mouth mirroring the lower plunging he was doing in an out of her wet heat. He stilled for her and looked into her dragon-green eyes.

"Will you marry me, Megan?" he asked.

"Yes!" she screamed and they exploded together in perfect unison.

CHAPTER 18

Megan sat eating plump red strawberries.

"Jesus, Meg, you're goin' ta stain yer dress," Josephine scolded her daughter.

"But they're so good and you know I like to eat when I'm nervous," she pouted.

Her mother looked at her though their reflection in the large mirror in front of them with love.

"You've nothin' ta be worried about love. You have a fine man there and I just know you'll be happy. Now stay still so I can fix yer veil."

The Belgian lace hung to the floor from a crown of red roses that adorned her ebony hair.

"You look beautiful," Gayle told her.

"So do you," she told her friend who was wearing a long silk burgundy gown. "You all do," she added for Diane and her mother who were in different dresses of the same color.

There was a knock at the door and then Uncle Ham poked his head in.

"I hate to rush you, ladies, but its bad luck to keep the groom waitin' too long. He caught a glimpse of Megan and his chest puffed up with pride.

"Are ya ready lass?" he asked her.

"Yes, I'm ready," she answered and walked toward his outstretched arm.

Snow lightly coated the ground as she made her way up to her father's church, her arm tucked in the crook of Ham's enormous one. They stood at the back and watched as her bridesmaids made their way down the aisle one by one. She was amazed that it had only taken a month to put the whole thing together and get everyone to Ireland. It was a miracle. The ends of each pew were all decorated with large sprays of roses and lilies that were expertly tied together with elegant satin bows. Two big candles were lit on either side of the altar and the big unity candle stood in the center.

She recalled the gasps of surprise when she had told everyone coming that it would be an evening wedding but she explained how it had special meaning to her and Gabe. The guest list was intimate and when everyone was seated the harpist switched from Ave Maria and began playing the wedding march.

"If you're goin' ta run you'd best do it now," Uncle Ham whispered in her ear.

"Not on your life," she said, smiling as she took the first step toward her future together with her angel.

During the long walk down the aisle, her eyes remained locked on Gabe's the entire time. He looked so handsome in his black tux and vest with his burgundy cravat. He had brushed his long hair back and it gleamed gold with an aura of red in the candlelight. When she and Ham reached him she handed her bouquet to Gayle. Ham took her arm from his and placed her hand in Gabe's. She saw him tear up a little as he gave her away.

"Take care of my girl or I'll crush you," he whispered bruskly.

They listened to the priest read solemnly and Megan could swear that as the moonlight shone down on them through the rose window, she could feel her father there with them giving his blessing.

They had both written their own vows and when it came time to read them Megan reached out to her mother she handed her the paper she had written hers on.

Her voice shook with emotion as she read; "Gabe, if ever two people were destined for one another I'd say it was us. You've opened my heart and filled it with love. You are my angel and I'm so grateful that I get to spend the rest of my life with you. I promise that I will love you forever for who you are. You are perfect to me."

"Megan, I didn't know what life was until I met you. I was an empty shell of a man who thought himself unworthy. Before you food had no taste, roses had no scent, touches brought no pleasure, sleep brought no dreams and life had no meaning. I was a cursed man until you came into my life. You are my miracle, my love, my soul, my heart, and my redemption. I am so honored that now I also get to call you my wife. I vow that I am yours forever."

The priest blessed them and they slid the symbols of their perfect unity, the rings, on each other's fingers and they were married. Cheers went up all around them and Gabe picked her up and carried her out of the church in his arms.

The newlyweds danced to their song in the ballroom of the castle, Gabe whispering naughty things in her ears and making her blush.

They had made sure to order things for the dinner that Gabe hadn't tried yet and he was stuffing himself at every turn he could.

They both watched raptly while her mother cried and hugged and talked to her brothers who all came to the wedding with their families.

"I guess anyone can be redeemed," Megan said and she truly believed it.

It seemed to be a season for miracles.

When it was time to cut the cake Megan giggled as he didn't go with the custom of her feeding him one bite and him doing the same for her but instead had pulled her on his lap and made her feed him the whole piece.

She sat with Diane and Gayle and as she and Diane chatted she noticed that Gayle had slipped a ring on her finger. Megan winked at her friend but kept talking to Diane until the need for distraction ended. The moment they stopped talking, Di looked at her hand and saw the big diamond winking at her in the candlelight.

"Will you marry me, Diane?" Gayle asked her.

"Of course!" she cried and wrapped her arms around her in an embrace.

"Well, I guess it's goin' around. Nothin' ta do about

it I suppose," Ham said and dropped to one knee beside where her mother sat.

"What the Christ are you doin' down there?" she asked him.

"I'm proposin' if ya shut up long enough ta let me," he said, exasperated.

"Well go on then," she said, sitting up straight and pushing her long red locks behind her shoulders.

"Josephine Black, will ya do me the honor of bein' my bride?" he asked as he pulled a small black box from his jacket pocket and opened it to reveal a round ruby in a gold setting.

"Oh, Ham ya big idiot. I thought you'd never ask!"

EPILOGUE

Megan and Gabe spent their honeymoon in Paris. Gabe took his new bride to the Eifel Tower along with every museum, gallery, and bakery there. Megan's favorite place was the Louvre, and her favorite piece turned out to be the Victory of Samothrace although she was in awe of the other masters displayed there.

"It must be the angel wings," she told Gabe when he pointed out that he assumed her favorite would be a painting.

Since they had opted to stay a whole month in France, Megan painted every chance she got. She did a lot of the city and scenery but she had found that her favorite subject was Gabriel. She'd force him to pose nude for her on a daily basis until too tempted to work. Then they'd make love until their stomachs would force them out for food.

Megan lay naked with her leg slung over him.

"You know there's supposed to be a wealth of information on Angels and Vampires here in France. Maybe there are even answers," she suggested.

"Maybe there are," he said and kissed her.

Did you like this story?

Stay tuned for more titles by **Aly Sebastian**

……and to find out what Megan and Gabe discover in the next book in the series, *Revelation*!

ABOUT THE AUTHOR

Aly is a writer and an artist. She works in the metaphysical field and uses that mysterious world and her unique perspective to enrich her writing. She lives in Massachusetts with her husband and three wonderful children.